KU-063-647

Enid Blyton®

Malory Towers

Winter Term

Written by Pamela Cox

*Hodder
Children's
Books*

HODDER CHILDREN'S BOOKS

First published in Great Britain in 2009 by Mammoth
This edition published in 2016 by Hodder and Stoughton Ltd

1 3 5 7 9 10 8 6 4 2

Text © Hodder and Stoughton, 2009
Cover illustration © Hodder and Stoughton
Enid Blyton's signature is a Registered Trade Mark of Hodder and Stoughton Ltd

Written by Pamela Cox

The moral right of the author has been asserted.

*All characters and events in this publication, other than those clearly
in the public domain, are fictitious and any resemblance to
real persons, living or dead, is purely coincidental.*

All rights reserved.
No part of this publication may be reproduced, stored in
a retrieval system, or transmitted, in any form or by any means, without
the prior permission in writing of the publisher, nor be otherwise circulated
in any form of binding or cover other than that in which it is published
and without a similar condition including this condition being
imposed on the subsequent purchaser.

A CIP catalogue record for this book
is available from the British Library.

ISBN 9781444929959

Printed and bound in Great Britain by
Printed and bound by Clays Ltd, St Ives plc

The paper and board used in this book
are made from wood from responsible sources

Hodder Children's Books
An imprint of
Hachette Children's Group
Part of Hodder and Stoughton
Carmelite House
50 Victoria Embankment
London EC4Y 0DZ

An Hachette UK Company
www.hachette.co.uk

www.hachettechildrens.co.uk

Contents

On the train

'Mother, there's Susan!' cried Felicity Rivers, as she and her mother made their way along the station platform. 'Susan! Hi, Susan!'

'Felicity, don't run!' called Mrs Rivers. 'It's far too crowded and you will bump into someone!'

But it was too late. Felicity was determined to reach her friend Susan and she ran along the platform, dodging the groups of people that stood here and there. Many of them were girls in the Malory Towers uniform, waiting for the train that would take them back to school for the winter term.

But Mrs Rivers was right, and it wasn't long before Felicity *did* bump into someone – a tall, red-haired girl with a serious expression and grey eyes.

'Felicity Rivers!' said the girl, looking rather cross. 'Do watch where you are going! And what do you mean by running around like a mad thing?'

'Sorry, Fenella,' said Felicity meekly, turning red. Of all the people she could have bumped into, why did she have to pick Fenella Thornton, the new Head Girl?

Fenella glared at her for a moment. Then, suddenly, her face broke into a wide smile, making her look quite different.

'Go on, push off!' she said with a chuckle. 'And this time, walk! Remember, you're a fourth former now, Felicity, not a silly little third former any more.'

Golly, so I am! thought Felicity, walking over to join Susan and her mother. Fancy *me* being a fourth former!

She and Susan greeted one another noisily, for they had to tell one another *everything* that had happened in the holidays. Then Mrs Rivers came up and chatted to Susan's mother, and at last it was time for the two girls to board the train.

Each of them hugged her mother, and Mrs Rivers said, 'Do write, won't you, darling? And I know that Darrell would love to hear from you, too.'

'I'll see you at half-term, dear,' said Susan's mother. 'Have a marvellous time!'

Felicity and Susan waved their mothers off, then grinned at one another as they walked down the train to find their carriage.

'The beginning of a new term,' said Susan. 'And now we are fourth formers!'

'Yes, we are, so why are you going towards the third-form carriage?' laughed Felicity, pulling her friend back. 'We don't want to sit with *those* babies!'

'Of course not,' said Susan loftily. 'Babies!'

Just then, the guard outside blew his whistle and, with a lurch, the train began to move forward slowly – on its way to Malory Towers!

'I say, isn't it exciting to be getting the train all on our own?' said Felicity.

'Much better than being in a stuffy old car,' agreed Susan.

The girls usually came to school by car, but Felicity's father had needed to drive to an urgent appointment, so she was getting the train for the first time. And, as she and Susan were quite inseparable, Susan's parents had agreed that she could catch the train with Felicity, too.

A sudden shout of laughter came from one of the carriages further along the train, and Felicity said, 'I'd know that laugh anywhere!'

'So would I,' grinned Susan. 'It's June!'

Quickly, Felicity and Susan made their way to the carriage that the laughter had come from, and slid open the door. And there, all chuckling their heads off, sat three of their fellow fourth formers – June, Freddie and Nora. There was another girl sitting in the corner of the carriage too, one that the girls hadn't seen before, but she wasn't laughing. In fact, her expression was very sullen indeed.

Heavens, she doesn't look very friendly, thought Felicity. I do hope that she isn't in North Tower with us.

The new girl, who was rather plain, with straight, mousey-brown hair, which fell to her shoulders, looked up as Felicity and Susan took their seats. Then she looked away again almost immediately, without so much as smiling at the newcomers. The two girls looked at one another and grimaced, but there was no time to worry about the new girl now, for their friends were welcoming them noisily.

'Hallo there, you two! Had good hols?'

'Isn't it grand to be going back to good old Malory Towers?'

'And this time we shall be in the fourth form! My goodness, we *are* going up in the world!'

'I don't know that I want to be a fourth former,' said Nora, frowning a little. 'We shall have to settle down a little and be more responsible now that we are in the upper school. It won't be nearly as much fun!'

The sullen-looking girl, who had been huddled miserably in the corner, looking out of the window, turned her head again at this, and threw Nora a scornful look. Fortunately, Nora didn't see it, but Felicity did, and felt quite shocked. Whatever had Nora done to deserve *that*?

'I have no intention at all of settling down,' said June. 'I don't see why we can't have a little fun, just because we are fourth formers.'

'Quite right!' said her friend, Freddie. 'We can still play the odd trick . . .'

'And have the occasional joke,' put in June.

'And, perhaps, we might even arrange a midnight feast!' said Freddie, her blue eyes lighting up.

The eyes of Felicity, Susan and Nora lit up too. A midnight feast would be simply too marvellous for words! They hadn't had one for absolutely ages. On the other hand, though, what Nora had said was quite true. The girls *were* expected to settle down a little once they were in the fourth form. But then Felicity remembered that when her sister Darrell had been in the upper fourth, they had held a feast. And if it was good enough for Darrell, it was good enough for Felicity!

'Perhaps we *could* have a feast,' she said, grinning. 'It's not as if we would be doing any harm. And as long as we keep it to ourselves, we can't be accused of setting a bad example to the lower forms.'

'My sentiments exactly!' cried June, clapping her on the back. 'My word, we're in for some fun this term.'

June's wicked, dark eyes were shining. She and Freddie were the jokers of the form, and fun was never far away when they were around!

'There's a very mischievous look about you this term, June,' said Susan, watching the girl.

'June *always* looks mischievous,' laughed Nora.

'Yes, but she looks even more mischievous than usual,' said Susan. 'And so do you, Freddie! Secretly planning lots of tricks, I expect!'

'Us?' said June, making her eyes very wide and innocent. 'Of course not!'

'As if we would!' said Freddie, also looking very innocent.

But the others knew that Freddie had spent the last few days of the holidays at June's. And June's brothers, who were also great jokers, had been there too. No doubt the two girls had come back with all kinds of jokes and tricks up their sleeves!

The new girl, who had sat in silence while the chatter went on around her, gave a sniff, and Felicity and Susan looked at the others enquiringly.

'Oh yes,' said June, as though she had only just

remembered that the girl was there. 'I haven't introduced you to our new member of the form, have I? This is Olive Witherspoon.'

Felicity and Susan said hallo, and the girl returned their greeting unsmilingly, in a tight little voice.

'Have you been to boarding school before, Olive?' asked Felicity, pleasantly.

'Yes,' said Olive shortly.

'Well, that's good,' said Susan, brightly. 'As you're used to it, I don't suppose you will feel too homesick, will you?'

'No,' came Olive's curt reply, and June muttered under her breath, 'Don't waste your time. She won't volunteer any information, and all you will get out of her are one-word answers. I gave up after about five minutes.'

'Yes, cheerful little soul, isn't she?' murmured Freddie.

Nora pulled a face and said in a low voice, 'Never mind about her! We've tried to be friendly, but she obviously doesn't want our company. Let's talk about something else instead. I say, did you know that Fenella Thornton has been made Head Girl, now that Kay Foster has left?'

'Yes, and old Amanda's gone, too,' said June. 'Ruth Grainger is taking her place as games captain.'

'I like Ruth,' said Freddie. 'And Fenella's not a bad sort, although she has a bit of a temper.'

'Yes, Fenella can be hot-tempered at times,' laughed Felicity. 'I bumped into her on the platform, quite literally! She was cross with me at first, but she soon got over it.'

'I wonder who will be head of the form?' said Susan.

'Well, it won't be me,' said Felicity. 'I had my turn in

the third form. I must say, I'm quite looking forward to taking a back seat this year.'

'And it certainly won't be me,' said June comfortably. 'I'm far too irresponsible.'

'And it won't be me, either,' laughed Freddie. 'For the same reason.'

'I'm much too scatterbrained,' said Nora. 'Potty and Miss Williams would never choose me.'

'Perhaps it will be Pam,' suggested Susan. 'She's so steady and good-tempered. And she was head girl when we were in the second form.'

'Pam was a super head-girl,' said Felicity. 'But I think that Miss Williams should give someone else a chance this term. It might be you, Susan!'

'No!' said June at once, with a horrified expression. 'Why, Susan would be no good at all as head-girl.'

'She would be marvellous!' retorted the normally even-tempered Felicity, firing up in defence of her friend. She had turned rather red, and June gave her a push, saying, 'Ass! I was only joking. Of course I know that Susan would be a splendid head-girl. I say, just imagine if Miss Williams made Bonnie head of the form? Or Amy?'

'I don't know which of them would be worse,' said Susan, with a shudder. 'It would certainly be an entertaining term if one of those two were chosen, but somehow I can't quite picture it happening!'

The chatter continued as the train went on its way, but still Olive took no part. Felicity, who thought that perhaps the girl was just very shy, felt a little sorry for her. Every now and then she tried to draw Olive into conversation, but, as before, the girl responded with terse answers, and asked no questions of her own.

She really was rather odd, decided Felicity, giving up. She remembered how excited she had felt about starting at Malory Towers, and how she had bombarded her older sister, Darrell, with questions. Yet Olive wasn't at all excited, and she didn't seem remotely curious about her new school either. It was very strange!

At last the train drew up at the little station near Malory Towers and, dragging their trunks and carrying their night cases, the girls alighted. Several big coaches were waiting to take the girls to the school, and Felicity and her friends boarded the first one, Olive following. Felicity and Susan sat together, of course, and so did June and Freddie. Which left Nora to sit next to the new girl, something which neither of them looked very pleased about.

Felicity and Susan felt sorry for Nora, for they would not have liked to sit next to the surly Olive either. They sat behind the two girls, and did their best to include Nora in their conversation, for which she was very grateful.

The coach journey was only a short one, and the girls grew very excited as the coach rounded a bend in the road, and their beloved Malory Towers came into view.

Felicity always loved this first glimpse of her school, thinking how magnificent it looked – almost like a castle, with its four towers, one at each corner.

In excitement, she cried out, 'Olive, look! There is Malory Towers, up on the cliff. Isn't it just the most beautiful building you have ever seen?'

Olive looked, but she made no comment. And Nora, stealing a sideways glance at the new girl, thought that her frown seemed to deepen.

There was great excitement as the coaches pulled up in the driveway, those girls who had arrived earlier by car gathering round to greet their friends.

'Felicity! I wondered where you were!'

'And there's Susan! Had good hols, Susan?'

'Hallo, June! And Freddie! My, isn't it good to be back?'

'Nora, old girl! Hurry up, and let's take our night cases to Matron.'

This was Nora's friend, the placid, even-tempered Pam. She looked with interest at Olive, who was coming down the steps behind Nora, and said in her friendly way, 'Hallo there! Welcome to Malory Towers. Are you going to be in the fourth form with us?'

'Yes,' answered Olive, in her funny, stiff little voice.

'Got your night case? Good, you can come along to Matron with the rest of us. I say, where did Felicity and Susan get to?'

Felicity and Susan had been swallowed up by a group of fourth formers. There was pretty little Bonnie, the haughty Amy, and freckle-faced Julie, with her friend, Lucy.

Julie and Lucy had brought their horses to school with them, and all of the girls were eager to go down to the stables and greet them.

'Thank goodness that there was room in the stables this term for Jack and Sandy,' said Felicity.

'Yes, it's wonderful to have him with me again,' said Julie. 'I don't blame Bill and Clarissa one little bit for what happened last term, of course, and I know that it won't happen again. But I just feel happier knowing that Jack is here, at Malory Towers.'

Last term there had been no room in the school stables for Jack and Sandy, so Julie and Lucy had stabled their horses at Five Oaks, a nearby riding school, which was run by two old girls. But there had been great consternation when Jack had gone missing. Fortunately, he had been found, and the culprit arrested, so everything had ended happily.

Now, though, Julie was even more reluctant to let Jack out of her sight than usual.

'Come along, everyone!' came Pam's voice from behind the little group. 'Let's take our health certificates to Matron and unpack our things. I'm simply dying to see our new dormitory and common-room.'

So the girls picked up their night cases and trooped inside North Tower to the big hall. A small group of first formers stood there, all of them looking nervous and a little lost.

'Poor little dears,' said Susan to Felicity. 'Shall we offer to take them upstairs to Matron?'

Felicity nodded, but before they had time to approach the first formers, a large, fair girl with a round face and very rosy cheeks strode up to them.

'Come on, kids!' she commanded, in a loud, very hearty voice. 'Follow me, and I'll take you to Matron's room. No lagging behind now!'

'Heavens, who's that?' asked Susan.

'Must be a new girl,' said June. 'Probably a fifth or sixth former by the look of her. I say, she looks like a mother duck, with all her little ducklings following behind her, doesn't she?'

The fourth formers burst out laughing, for that was exactly what the big girl did look like! Susan, however, was a little put out. It simply wasn't done for a new girl to be so bossy, and take charge of the young ones like that – even if she was a top former!

Just then, someone called out, 'Hallo, you kids! No loitering in the hall now, or I shall dish out a punishment.'

The girls turned to see a tall, graceful girl standing there, a wide smile on her face.

'Esme!' they cried. 'How marvellous to see you!'

Lucy, who was Esme's cousin, punched the girl gently on the shoulder, and said, 'I'm surprised that you even bother with us small fry now that you're a fifth former.'

'It's only because there's no one else around,' said Esme with a perfectly straight face. 'Of course, if I should happen to pass you when I'm with any of my form I shall simply walk past with my nose in the air.'

Then she laughed, and the others laughed with her, for they knew that Esme – who had been in their form last term – would never go all high-and-mighty on them, no matter what.

When the girls arrived at Matron's room, the big, fair-haired girl was there, still fussing over the first formers. Matron herself was looking rather irritated, but her stern face relaxed into a smile when she saw the fourth formers. 'All got your health certificates?' she said, in her brisk tone. 'Good. Now, I want no illnesses, and no broken bones this term. Is that clear?'

'Yes, Matron,' chorused the girls, all except Olive, who hung back and looked at Matron suspiciously. The others knew that Matron was only joking, and there was no one they would rather have look after them if they fell ill. But, to Olive, she seemed a most unsympathetic person. Matron noticed the girl watching her, and, looking at the list in her hand, said with a smile, 'You must be Olive Witherspoon. And I have another new girl here for the fourth form, too. Sylvia, come and meet the rest of your form.'

The girls followed Matron's gaze and realised, with surprise, that she was talking to the rather bossy girl who had borne the first formers off. Heavens, was she going to be in the fourth form too?

The first evening

The girl turned at once, and strode across to the others, a broad smile on her round face. 'How lovely to meet you all!' she boomed, in her hearty voice. 'I'm Sylvia Chalmers, and I'm so happy to be at Malory Towers. I was at St Hilda's until the end of last term, you know, but our Head was taken ill and it had to be closed down. So sad! It was a simply super school, but I'm sure that Malory Towers will be every bit as nice.'

Sylvia paused to take a breath, and Matron seized the chance to say, 'Well, Sylvia, the girls will show you and Olive to your dormitory, then you can all unpack.'

'Oh, I know where the dormitory is, Matron,' said Sylvia. 'I arrived early this morning, you know. And my things are already unpacked. I was just going to show the youngsters to their dormitory, because I always like to help out if I can.' She beamed round at the others, who were all staring at her open-mouthed. Heavens, what a chatterbox!

Bonnie put a hand to her forehead, and murmured to Amy, 'I'm beginning to get a headache.'

'Oh, poor you!' said Sylvia, whose sharp ears had caught this. 'My mother suffers dreadfully from headaches, so I know just what you should do! You need to take –'

But Bonnie never found out what she needed to take, for Matron, quite affronted, cut in, to say crisply, 'Thank you, Sylvia, but *I* am Matron of North Tower, and if Bonnie has a headache she can come to me for a remedy.'

Then she reached up and took a large bottle of green medicine down from one of her shelves, shaking it in Bonnie's direction. 'A dose of this will cure your headache, Bonnie,' she said.

But, miraculously, Bonnie found that her headache had suddenly disappeared!

'I thought it might,' said Matron drily, putting the bottle back on her shelf. 'Now, off you go, all of you, for the first day of term is a very busy one for me, and you are all in my way.'

The fourth formers went out, but Sylvia lingered, saying, 'Matron, I was hoping that I might show the first formers where their dormitory is, and help them to settle in.'

Matron, who was growing a little tired of Sylvia and her pushy manner, said firmly, 'The first formers can learn to find their own way around, Sylvia. They certainly don't need you chivvying them round. Now do, please, go and join the others.'

'Well, what a know-it-all!' said Nora, as the rest of the fourth form made their way along the corridor.

'Isn't she just?' said Susan. 'And she acts as if she has been at Malory Towers for years, not just a few hours.'

'I can see that she's going to be jolly trying,' said Felicity. 'I wonder how she knows her way around so well?'

'You can ask her,' said June. 'Here she comes!'

And, when Sylvia caught up with them, Felicity *did* ask her.

'Oh, whenever I go anywhere new, I always make a point of exploring, so that I can find my way around,' explained Sylvia in her loud voice. 'I do so hate having to ask where I'm supposed to be going all the time, don't you?'

Felicity opened her mouth to answer, but Sylvia swept on, 'It can be quite uncomfortable being the new girl, among so many others who have been here for a long time, especially when you have been used to being *somebody* at your old school.'

'*Somebody?*' repeated Julie, with rather a dazed expression.

'Oh yes, I was head-girl in several forms at my old school,' said Sylvia airily. 'I'm afraid I do have rather a tendency to rule the roost.'

'Really?' said June in a smooth little voice. 'I would never have guessed.'

The others giggled, and before Sylvia could hold forth again, Susan said, 'Well, let's get along to our dormitory, or we shan't have time to see anything before tea.' Then, in a lower tone, she murmured to Felicity, 'My word, if Sylvia tries to rule the roost in the fourth form she'll be in for a shock!'

Indeed she would, thought Felicity, smiling to herself. There were several very strong characters in the fourth, and they would have no hesitation in putting Sylvia in her place if she became too bossy!

The fourth-form dormitory was a very pleasant room, large and airy, with cream-painted walls. Each bed had a brightly coloured bedspread on it, and a locker beside it, so that the girls had somewhere to keep their personal belongings.

Sylvia, of course, had already unpacked and arranged several things on top of her locker, and she hovered round the others now, saying brightly, 'If anyone wants a hand with their unpacking, they only have to say the word.'

'If they can get one in edgeways,' muttered June darkly, making the others laugh.

Olive, in complete contrast to Sylvia, had remained very much in the background and, as the fourth formers entered their dormitory, Felicity turned to the girl.

'Settling in all right?' she asked, with a smile.

Olive merely nodded, and Felicity, determined to draw her out, tried again, asking, 'Which school did you go to before you came here?'

'Chartley Manor,' answered Olive.

'What made you leave and come to Malory Towers?' asked Susan, coming over to help Felicity in her efforts.

And, quite suddenly, Olive's face lost its sullen, uninterested expression, becoming angry and red, as she hissed at Susan, 'Mind your own business!'

Then she turned away, flung her night case on to the nearest bed and began furiously pulling things out.

'Well!' said Susan, annoyed and rather shaken. 'What on earth brought that outburst on? Of all the nerve! Olive can remain in her shell now, for all I care! I certainly won't bother trying to make conversation with her again.'

Felicity, angry on her friend's behalf, glared at Olive. But the girl kept her head down as she concentrated on her unpacking, and didn't even notice.

'I've a jolly good mind to go and tell her what I think of her!' said Felicity, her cheeks glowing red.

But Susan said, 'Don't let's bother about her, Felicity. I'm certainly not going to let her spoil our first day back at school. Besides, at least I managed to get *four* words out of her, instead of just one!'

Felicity laughed at this, but she still felt sore with the new girl, sitting as far away from her as possible at the tea table later.

The girls rubbed their hands together happily as they went into the dining-room, Nora sniffing the air appreciatively. 'Sausages and mash, with gravy, unless I'm much mistaken,' she said. 'And treacle sponge for pudding. Yummy!'

Mam'zelle Dupont, the plump little French mistress, was already at the head of the fourth-form table when the girls seated themselves, and she smiled round, delighted to see everyone again, crying, '*Bonjour, mes enfants!*'

The fourth formers were very fond of Mam'zelle, and smiled back. But they didn't have a chance to return her greeting, for, once again, Sylvia pushed herself forward, saying brightly, '*Bonjour*, Mam'zelle! I'm Sylvia Chalmers, and we met earlier.'

'Ah yes,' began Mam'zelle. 'I remember. Miss Potts –'

'Miss Potts introduced us,' interrupted Sylvia. 'And you

and I had a lovely, long chat about France, for I spent my summer holiday there, and I was telling you all about it.'

Mam'zelle's smile began to slide a little, and she murmured, '*Oui* – it was a very, *very* long chat indeed.'

'I simply must show you the photographs I took, Mam'zelle,' Sylvia chattered on. Then she looked round the table, and said, 'I'm sure that you would all find them most interesting, girls. You see, we stayed in the most beautiful chateau, and . . .'

Then, to Sylvia's astonishment, the fourth formers all began to talk to one another, very loudly and very pointedly. Even Mam'zelle turned away and began to talk rapidly to Nora, taking care not to meet Sylvia's eye again.

As for Sylvia herself, she began to eat her sausages and mashed potato, feeling puzzled and a little hurt. She wanted *so* badly to fit in here, and really had gone out of her way to be friendly. Poor Sylvia! She simply couldn't see that she was trying just a little *too* hard.

It was a strange meal, thought Felicity. Normally the fourth formers would have pointed out all the mistresses to the new girls, telling them which ones to beware of, and which ones were easy to get round, or good to play tricks on. But Olive didn't seem in the slightest bit interested, while Sylvia seemed to know all there was to know already!

Just then, June glanced towards the first-form table, and noticed that there was a new mistress sitting there, beside Miss Potts, the head of North Tower.

'I wonder who that is, with Miss Potts?' she said, and

the others turned to look. The mistress looked very young, and had tightly curled blonde hair, which looked very striking with her dark brows and brown eyes.

'Do you know who she is, Sylvia?' asked June.

'Of course not,' said Sylvia, rather defensively. 'Why should I?'

'Well, you seem to know everything else,' said June.

'She looks awfully young,' said Nora. 'I wonder what she is going to teach?'

'Ah, I know who this new mistress must be!' cried Mam'zelle, who had been listening, and surveying the new teacher with great interest. 'Perhaps you do not know, *mes filles*, but our good Miss Hibbert was taken ill during the holidays, and has been ordered to stay at home and rest.'

The fourth formers were sorry to hear this, for Miss Hibbert, who taught English and Drama, was an excellent teacher, with a knack of making her lessons very interesting indeed.

'That's bad news!' said Felicity, looking very grave. 'I do hope that there is nothing seriously wrong with Miss Hibbert, Mam'zelle?'

'*Non*, but she must not return to Malory Towers until she has fully recovered,' said the French mistress. 'That is why Miss Grayling has engaged someone else to take her place this term. Her name, I think, is Miss Tallant.'

'She's very pretty,' said Bonnie, surveying the mistress critically.

'In a rather common sort of way,' said Amy with a sniff. 'I bet her hair is dyed.'

'She looks as if she might be good fun,' said Lucy. 'The younger mistresses often are.'

'I think she looks rather hard,' said June to Freddie, in a low voice that could not be overheard by Mam'zelle. 'Mark my words, our Miss Tallant is going to be trouble, and not fun at all!'

Olive, meanwhile, sat silently and ate very little, merely pushing the food around her plate. She wasn't interested in the new mistress. She didn't like Malory Towers. And she didn't like the girls! Not that nosy Susan, nor snobbish Amy, and certainly not the bossy Sylvia. As for Nora and Bonnie, they were both the kind of girls that Olive disliked most, with their big eyes, pretty faces and sweet, innocent expressions. Olive knew all about girls like them. She knew how they used their sweetness and prettiness to get their own way, and to make themselves the centre of attention. While plainer girls, like Olive herself, had to find other ways to make themselves noticed, or be ignored altogether.

Certainly the new girl had not made any impression on Mam'zelle, who had barely noticed that she was there. Felicity suddenly realised, with a pang of guilt, that no one had bothered to introduce Olive to the French mistress. Really, she thought, it was quite Olive's own fault if she was left out of things, for she had made no effort at all to respond to the others' attempts at making friends. All the same, someone ought to make the introduction, and as Felicity had been head of the form last year, she decided that it was up to her.

'Mam'zelle,' she said. 'I don't think that you've met our other new girl, Olive Witherspoon.'

'Ah, you are so quiet, *ma petite*, that I did not notice you!' said Mam'zelle, smiling at the girl. 'Well, these fourth formers will make you welcome, for they are good girls, and soon you will be just like them.'

Just then, Bonnie let out a squeal that made everyone jump, and leapt up from her chair, wailing, 'Oh no, I've spilled my tea all over my skirt!'

'You are scalded, *ma chère*!' cried Mam'zelle dramatically, getting to her feet. 'I shall take you to Matron at once!'

'I'm not scalded, Mam'zelle, for the tea was almost cold,' said Bonnie, dabbing rather ineffectually at the damp patch on her skirt with a handkerchief. 'It was just such a shock, that's all. Thank heavens I have another skirt in my trunk. Amy, be a dear and pour me another cup of tea, would you?'

How typical, thought Olive, watching the little by-play with a sour expression. Bonnie was quite obviously one of Mam'zelle's favourites, and the girl simply couldn't bear to see the French mistress paying attention to someone else. So she had purposely spilled her tea in her lap and then made a big – and quite unnecessary – fuss about it. Olive's lip curled scornfully and, seeing this, Felicity nudged Susan, murmuring, 'Just look at Olive's face! It's enough to turn the milk sour!'

In fact, Olive was being extremely unjust, for Bonnie had been deep in conversation with Amy, and hadn't even realised that Mam'zelle was speaking to Olive. Nor had she spilled the tea on purpose, for it really *had* been an accident.

But the new girl had taken a completely irrational dislike to both Bonnie and Nora, and it came to the fore again when the girls were relaxing in the common-room that evening.

'I must say, this is a jolly nice common-room,' said Sylvia, whose hurt silence at the tea-table had lasted all of five minutes. She liked the sound of her own voice far too much to be quiet for any longer! 'Very cosy! I'm sure we shall have some wonderful times in here, all chattering away together!'

'What Sylvia means is that *she* will chatter, while *we* are forced to listen to her,' muttered Amy under her breath, scowling at the new girl. 'I think it's dreadfully vulgar, the way that she pushes herself to the fore all the time!'

'Of course, when I was head of the form at St Hilda's, we used to have all kinds of fun and games in the common-room,' the new girl went on. 'I organised most of them myself, for if there is one thing I pride myself on it's being a good organiser. And, if I do say so myself, I'm jolly good at thinking up games to play. I could show you some of them, if you like, and . . .'

'Thanks. If we ever feel that we need someone to organise us, or tell us what to do in our free time, we'll let you know,' said June, with heavy sarcasm.

But Sylvia was too thick-skinned to recognise sarcasm, and she continued to talk and talk and talk! At last it became too much for Nora, who jumped up and put a gramophone record on.

'Good show, Nora!' called out Freddie.

Then, to the amusement of the fourth formers, Nora began to do a little tap dance in the middle of the floor.

'You're full of beans tonight!' said Pam, in surprise. 'Usually it's all you can do to keep your eyes open after the journey back to Malory Towers.'

'Ah yes, but I have been staying at my aunt's, and she doesn't live many miles from here, so it was only a short drive back,' explained Nora, stopping in mid-dance. 'So I feel quite wide awake, for once!'

'You're not a bad dancer, Nora,' said Sylvia – rather patronisingly, the others thought. In fact, Nora, who was naturally graceful, was a very good dancer and had been taking lessons in the holidays. She opened her mouth to tell the others this, but Sylvia got in first, saying, 'I simply love dancing, and, if I do say so myself, I have quite a talent for it.'

'My gosh, can you imagine it?' muttered Lucy, under her breath. 'It would be like watching a baby elephant!'

This was a little unkind, but Julie couldn't help laughing, and Sylvia, quite oblivious, went on, 'I coached some of the youngsters in dancing, for their part in the school concert last year, and it all went swimmingly. The parents thought that it was marvellous, and I do think that I have a knack for teaching people things, even if –'

'Even if you do say so yourself,' interrupted June smoothly, as muffled laughter ran round the room.

Sylvia looked a little puzzled at this, and while she was temporarily lost for words, Nora cried, 'Let me show you all a dance I learned in the holidays. Turn the music up, Felicity.'

Felicity obeyed, and the others moved back to make room for Nora. Then they watched, entranced, as she danced for them, her movements very graceful and balletic. Nora was a complete scatterbrain, and a bit of a duffer at most of her lessons, so it was very nice to see her excel at something, thought Felicity.

As Nora curtseyed daintily, the fourth formers clapped and cheered. All except Olive, who sat with her arms folded, her mouth set in a thin line and an expression of scorn on her face.

Susan, who still felt angry with the girl because of her earlier outburst, nudged Olive rather sharply and said, 'What's the matter with you? You could at least join us in clapping Nora.'

'Why should I?' said Olive sullenly. 'Nora is a show-off, and I don't like show-offs!'

The others gasped and muttered angrily, Pam saying hotly, 'How dare you, Olive! You take that back at once!'

'I shan't,' said Olive obstinately. 'She *is* a show-off, and so is Bonnie! Both of them have to be the centre of attention, all the time.'

Poor little Bonnie looked quite stunned, for she couldn't think what she had done to make the new girl dislike her so. Why, she had barely exchanged more than a few words with her.

'I see what it is!' said Amy, suddenly. 'You're jealous. Bonnie and Nora are both pretty, and dainty, while as for you ...' The girl paused as she looked Olive up and down, rather scornfully. 'Well, no one could call *you* pretty!'

Olive turned pale, and shrank back as though Amy had struck her. Everyone else was quiet, for – although Nora and Bonnie felt grateful to Amy for sticking up for them – most of the girls felt that she had gone a little too far. Olive *was* very plain, but it had been rather cruel to point it out in front of everyone like that.

'That's enough!' said Felicity sharply. 'There are only five minutes until bedtime, so let's not waste them in arguing.'

'Well done,' said Susan, grinning at Felicity, as everyone dispersed. 'Once a head-girl, always a head-girl!'

Felicity laughed and said, 'Well, *someone* had to take charge, before things got out of hand. I must say, though, that I think we've been rather unlucky in our new girls this term.'

'Haven't we just!' agreed Susan. 'Olive is a real misery, and I'm afraid it looks as if she's going to be rather spiteful, too. And Sylvia is simply too pushy for words! She'll try and take over everything if we aren't careful.'

Felicity nodded, and said, 'I've a feeling that this is going to be quite a difficult term!'

Exciting news

After breakfast the following day, all of the new girls had to go and see Miss Grayling, the Head mistress. Fenella Thornton, the Head Girl, rounded them all up from the four towers and took them along to the Head's study.

There were six girls altogether, from various forms, most of them looking a little nervous as Fenella lead them to Miss Grayling's room. Olive, wearing her habitual sulky expression, walked a little way behind the rest, dragging her feet. She hadn't wanted to come to this stupid school in the first place, and she couldn't think that anything the Head mistress had to say would be of the slightest interest to her. Sylvia, on the other hand, was very eager to meet Miss Grayling, and felt quite certain that she would make a good impression on her.

She strode along confidently beside Fenella, and said brightly, 'I've heard that Miss Grayling is a wonderful person.'

'She is,' said Fenella. 'There is no one I would rather go to if I was in any kind of trouble, and –'

'Our headmistress at St Hilda's was just the same,' cut in Sylvia. 'So wise and kind.' Fenella, who was not accustomed to being interrupted when she spoke to a lower-form girl, looked rather taken aback. A sharp retort sprang to her lips, then she reminded herself that Sylvia was new and rather over-enthusiastic, so she held her tongue.

But even Sylvia was silent in the presence of Miss Grayling. The Head was a calm, dignified woman, with a rather serious face, which could, at times, break into the most beautiful smile. She could also be very stern indeed, when the need arose, and although Miss Grayling looked perfectly serene now, each of the new girls hoped fervently that they would never be called before her for misbehaviour!

Fenella left the room, and the Head spoke to each girl individually, asking her name and form. Even Olive found that she did not dare address Miss Grayling in her usual, surly manner, and answered politely. But she still looked rather miserable, and the Head stared at her hard. She knew far more about Olive Witherspoon than that young lady realised! Sylvia, for once, was quite subdued, and confined herself to answering the questions that Miss Grayling asked her, rather than chattering endlessly about herself.

Then the Head addressed the group as a whole, saying gravely, 'One day you will leave school, and go out into the world as young women. You should take with you a good understanding of many things, along with a willingness to accept responsibility and help others. I do not count as our successes those who have won scholarships and passed exams, though these are worthy achievements. I count as our successes those who learn to be good-hearted and kind, sensible and trustworthy – good, sound women the world can lean on.'

The six girls before Miss Grayling listened intently, her words making a great impression on them. Sylvia felt quite determined to become one of Malory Towers' successes.

Olive was quite certain that *she* would not be one. But Miss Grayling's words were so inspiring that, just for a moment, she wished that she could be.

By the time that the new girls joined the others, in the fourth-form class-room, all of the seats had been taken, apart from three, side-by-side, in the front row. Another new girl called Sarah, who was in East Tower, quickly slipped into the one nearest the window, leaving the two North Tower girls to take the others.

'I think that Sylvia and Olive are going to be thrown together quite a lot,' said Susan to Felicity, as the new girls slipped into the empty seats. 'They are the only two who don't have a special friend to pair up with.'

'Well, perhaps they will be good for one another,' said Felicity. 'In spite of her faults, Sylvia seems jolly and good-hearted, so perhaps some of that will rub off on to Olive.'

'Let's hope so,' said Susan. 'And, with a bit of luck, Olive might quieten Sylvia down a little.'

'Shh!' hissed Freddie, who was standing by the door. 'Miss Williams is coming!'

At once everyone stopped talking and stood up very

straight, while Freddie politely held the door open for the fourth-form mistress.

Miss Williams thanked her, and walked to the big desk at the front of the class. She was a scholarly woman, with a rather prim appearance and a gentle manner. But she also had a quiet air of authority, and certainly knew how to keep her class in order.

'Good morning, girls,' she said, smiling round.

'Good morning, Miss Williams,' chorused the girls.

'Please sit down. Now, before we get on with the business of making out timetables and handing out books, there are one or two things that I have to say to you.'

'I bet that she's going to announce who will be head of the form!' whispered Nora to Pam.

'Quiet please, Nora,' said Miss Williams, without raising her voice.

Heavens, thought Felicity, she must have awfully sharp ears, for Nora sat near the back of the class.

'First of all,' began the mistress, 'I am sure that you are all eager to know who is to be head-girl of the fourth form.'

Everyone sat up straight in their seats, and Miss Williams went on, 'I consulted Miss Potts and Miss Peters before making a decision, and, in the end, we all agreed that we would like to try Susan Blake.'

A cheer went up, and those nearest to Susan patted her on the back, while Felicity cried, 'Well done, old girl! You'll be first-rate, I just know it.'

Susan, who had turned quite pink with pleasure, could

hardly speak for a moment, then, at last, she said, 'Thank you, Miss Williams. You won't regret your decision, I promise you. I shall do my very best.'

'I am quite sure that you will,' said the mistress, smiling at the girl. 'And now, I have something else to tell you all. At the end of the term, the three top forms will be putting on a Christmas concert, which the parents will be coming to watch. The concert will last for approximately an hour and a half, so each form will have to fill half an hour. It is entirely up to you what you choose to do – sing carols, recite, or perform a short play. But I want every member of the form involved in some way, either as a performer, or behind the scenes.'

The fourth formers looked at one another, absolutely thrilled, as an excited murmur ran round the class. My word, what fun this was going to be! Each of the girls was absolutely determined that their contribution to the concert, whatever it was, would far outshine the fifth and sixth formers.

Miss Williams smiled at the girls' enthusiasm and went on, 'Susan, as head-girl, you will be in charge of the whole project, of course. And I am quite sure that you will have no shortage of willing helpers.'

There was no doubt about that! Half a dozen voices cried, 'We'll help you all right, Susan!'

Sylvia was just as excited and interested as the others. Why, at her old school she had produced a play and it had been a roaring success. If only Susan would hand over the reins and let her, Sylvia, produce the fourth's contribution to the Christmas concert, she would really be able to show the others what she could do!

Miss Williams rapped on the desk with a ruler and said, 'Well, I'm very pleased that you are all so eager. But we really must settle down and get on with more mundane matters. However, before we do so, I should just mention that we have a new English and Drama teacher this term. Her name is Miss Tallant, and she will be replacing Miss Hibbert for a little while. Miss Tallant will, of course, be happy to give you – and the other forms – any help that you require with your contribution to the concert.'

'Thank you, Miss Williams,' said Susan, whose head was in a perfect whirl. 'It's nice to know that there is someone we can call on if we need advice.'

The fourth formers crowded round Susan at break-time.

'I say, what a marvellous term this is going to be!'

'I simply can't wait to get started on our piece for the concert.'

'Yes, we'll show the fifth and sixth formers how it should be done, all right!'

'Well, we'd better have a meeting in the common-room, after prep this evening,' said Susan. 'Bring plenty of ideas with you, everyone, for we shall need them.'

'We'd better find out what the fifth and sixth formers intend to do as well,' said Felicity. 'I mean to say, it will be no use if all three forms decide to sing carols, or something. That will be terribly boring for the audience.'

'Yes, you're right,' said Susan. 'Well, I'll have to have a word with Fenella, and Katie Ellis, who is head of the fifth, then we can all make sure that we are doing different things.'

So, when the fourth formers gathered for their meeting that evening, Susan was armed with the necessary information.

The girls sat on the chairs and sofas, while Susan perched on the edge of a table, a notebook and pen in her hand. There was a good deal of excited chatter going on, and Susan clapped her hands together for silence.

'Well,' she began. 'I've found out that the fifth form are going to sing carols, and the sixth are planning to do a selection of Christmas readings.'

'Sounds a bit dry,' said Freddie, pulling a face.

'That's exactly what I thought,' said Susan, with a grin. 'Though, of course, I didn't say that to Katie and Fenella!'

'So, it looks as if it's up to us fourth formers to add a little fun to the proceedings,' said June, looking thoughtful.

'I say!' said Julie. 'Remember that splendid pantomime that Darrell, Alicia and the others put on when they were in the fifth? Wouldn't it be marvellous if we could do something like that?'

'We could never squeeze a whole pantomime into half an hour,' said Felicity.

'No, it would be impossible,' said Pam. 'Besides, super though their pantomime was, I don't think that any of us really want to copy Darrell and the others. It would be much better if we came up with a completely original idea.'

There were murmurs of agreement, and Nora piped up,

'How about a display of dancing? We could all dress up as fairies, and angels, and what-not, and . . .'

'And you could take centre-stage,' said Olive, with a sneer.

Nora turned bright red, stung by the injustice of this. She had made the suggestion because of her love of dancing, but she certainly wasn't the kind of person who wanted to steal the limelight all the time! Fortunately, the others knew her well enough to realise this, and Susan said coolly, 'Do you have any ideas about what we could do as our contribution to the concert, Olive?'

'No,' muttered Olive, sulkily.

'I thought as much. Well, if you don't have anything useful to say, kindly keep quiet.'

Then Susan turned to Nora and said, 'Thanks for the suggestion, but most of us can't dance as well as you can, so I really don't think it would work. We need something that we can all be involved in.'

'What about putting on a short play?' said Felicity. 'There are lots of scripts for plays in the library, so we could try and find one with a Christmassy theme.'

This sounded more like it, and the girls looked at one another excitedly.

'Marvellous idea!' cried June. 'And if we can find something that has a bit of humour in it, so much the better.'

Sylvia, who had been unusually silent, perked up at this and said, 'That sounds super! We put a play on at St Hilda's once, and it brought the house down. Of course, I produced it, and –'

'And I expect you wrote it yourself, too, didn't you?' said Freddie.

'Oh no, though I did add a few lines of my own,' said Sylvia, looking pleased at Freddie's apparent interest. 'You see –'

'I bet you designed all the costumes,' put in Bonnie.

'And painted the scenery yourself,' said Lucy.

'And probably took the leading role, too,' said Nora.

'Oh no, that would have been far too much work for just one person!' said the thick-skinned Sylvia, still completely unaware that the others were making fun of her. 'Naturally I supervised everything, for I think it's so important to have someone in charge who can organise things, and see that they go smoothly. And everything really did go like clockwork, if I do say so myself.'

'If she says that once more, I shall go mad,' muttered Amy savagely, while Susan went on smoothly, 'I do so agree with you, Sylvia. It's *very* important to have someone who can organise things at the helm. And, as Miss Williams has put me in charge, *I* am that someone. But that doesn't mean to say that I intend to go all bossy on you, and take over everything. This is going to be *our* play, and I will welcome any sensible suggestions, and listen to them.'

That was the right way to run things, thought Felicity. Susan was firm, yet not the slightest bit domineering, and she was determined that this was going to be a form effort.

'We really need to decide on a play as quickly as possible,' said Pam. 'We can't start casting parts, or deciding who is going to do what, until that has been sorted out.'

'Right,' said Susan. 'So, what I suggest is that as many of us as possible go along to the library over the next few days, and read through some of the scripts that are stored there. If anyone finds anything that they think might be suitable, please bring it to me. Then we'll hold another meeting in here on Saturday, and make a decision.'

'Good show!' someone called out, and Susan grinned.

'That's just what I hope it will be,' she said. 'A good show. The best show that Malory Towers has ever seen!'

The new mistress

Soon the old girls felt as if they had been back at school for weeks, not just days. Sylvia, too, settled down in her own way, though she often irritated the others with her never-ending chatter, and the way she always tried to take the lead.

This was particularly galling to Felicity, Susan and June, who had always been the leaders of their form, and the three of them often found it necessary to put Sylvia in her place.

'I thought that June was going to explode yesterday, when Sylvia took it upon herself to show her the best way to hold her lacrosse stick,' said Felicity, smiling, as she remembered.

Susan grinned too, and said, 'She *will* explode, one day, if Sylvia keeps it up. And I can't honestly say that I blame her! Sylvia is such an expert on everything – even things she's not very good at, like lacrosse.'

'It's difficult to dislike her wholeheartedly, though,' said Felicity, looking thoughtful. 'She's annoying, but she doesn't have any mean, petty faults.'

'Unlike dear Olive,' said Susan, with a sigh. 'Who has so many mean, petty faults that it is quite impossible to like her!'

'I really don't think I've ever met anyone so unfriendly in my life,' Felicity said. 'I tried to start a friendly conversation with her in the dorm yesterday morning, just to see if I could get through to her, and almost got my head bitten off!'

Felicity had seen the girl putting a photograph on her bedside cabinet, and went over to take a look. It was a picture of Olive, with a man and woman, whom Felicity took to be her parents. Her mother and father were smiling happily, but Olive's mouth was set in its usual, sullen droop.

'Are these your parents?' asked Felicity, pleasantly.

'That's my father,' Olive answered flatly. 'And my stepmother.'

As Felicity leaned forward to take a closer look, she noticed something odd about the photograph. Mr Witherspoon had his right arm out at an odd angle, as if he had it around someone's shoulders. But there was no one on his right side at all. In fact, the edge of the photograph was jagged, as if a piece had been torn off.

'There's someone missing,' said Felicity, mildly curious. And Olive's temper had flared up at once.

'No, there isn't!' she had cried. 'I tore part of the photograph off so that I could fit it into the frame, that's all. Not that it has anything to do with you – interfering little busybody!' With that, Olive had snatched up the photograph and flung it into her bedside cabinet, slamming the door shut.

'I wish I had never been sent to this beastly school!' she

raged, angry tears starting to her eyes. 'I knew exactly how it would be, with everyone poking their noses into my private business!'

Felicity was quite flabbergasted, of course. She hadn't meant to pry at all, and had only been making polite conversation. Just as she was on the verge of giving the new girl a thorough dressing-down for her rudeness, Felicity received some unexpected support.

'Pooh!' said a small, lisping voice. 'Who on earth is interested in *your* business, Olive?'

It was Bonnie, of course, her little nose wrinkled in disdain, as she went on, 'I think that you are quite the rudest girl I have ever met.'

Olive had turned on Bonnie, saying scornfully, 'Do you think I care what people like *you* think of me? Why, you're nothing but a silly, babyish little doll!'

'*Doll?*' Bonnie had squeaked. '*Doll?* How dare you! Do you know, Olive, I'm beginning to think that Amy was right, and you are jealous! I can't think of any other reason why you dislike me so much.'

And Bonnie had flounced off, while Felicity said to Olive, 'I'd be careful, if I were you. Bonnie is nowhere near as silly as you seem to imagine, and she can be a dangerous enemy. Watch out, Olive!'

But Olive had merely shrugged, so Felicity had left her to it, thinking that it was just impossible to help some people.

'Yes, she's a strange one, all right,' said Susan now. 'And I, for one, am quite tired of her and her unpleasant ways.'

'Let's not waste any more time talking about her, then,' said Felicity, slipping her arm through Susan's. 'We have our first Drama lesson with the new mistress shortly. That should be interesting.'

As it turned out, it was a *very* interesting lesson indeed!

Bonnie held the door open for Miss Tallant, as she entered the class-room, and gave the mistress one of her sweet smiles. Miss Tallant smiled back, and went to the front of the class, her dark, dramatic eyes sweeping round.

The girls eyed her just as keenly, for they had never seen a teacher quite like Miss Tallant before. Most of the mistresses at Malory Towers dressed neatly and sensibly, in quite plain clothes. The new mistress, though, was wearing a flowing, brightly patterned skirt and a very fussy blouse, with lots of frills. She also wore big, dangling earrings, which swung to and fro every time she moved her head, and Pam murmured to Nora, 'Heavens! She looks as if she has a couple of dinner gongs hanging from her ears!'

Nora gave one of her explosive snorts of laughter, and Miss Tallant turned her head.

'Do you find something amusing?' she asked softly, a smile on her face.

'N-no, Miss Tallant,' stammered Nora, looking rather apprehensive now. 'I'm sorry, I didn't mean –'

'Stand up when you address me,' said the mistress, still in the same calm voice, and still smiling.

Very red now, Nora got to her feet, and Miss Tallant asked, 'What is your name?'

'Nora Woods, Miss Tallant,' answered poor Nora.

The mistress's smile grew wider, and she said, 'Well, Nora Woods, it might interest you to know that I don't stand for any nonsense in my classes. Come and see me after the lesson, and I will think of a suitable punishment for you. Sit down.'

A gasp ran round the class as Miss Tallant turned to face the blackboard, and a great many sympathetic glances were sent in Nora's direction. But nobody dared to speak to the girl, for fear that they would be punished too.

The mistress turned to Bonnie, her ridiculously large earrings swinging, and she asked, 'What is your name, my dear?'

'Bonnie Meadows, Miss Tallant,' lisped Bonnie, her wide gaze fixed admiringly on the mistress.

'Bonnie, please hand these round to everyone,' said Miss Tallant, indicating a pile of books on her desk. 'As quickly as you can, there's a good girl.'

Nimbly, Bonnie skipped round the room, handing a book to each girl, before returning to her seat.

'Thank you,' said Miss Tallant, smiling at her with approval. 'Now, girls, we are going to begin reading a play. You will all take it in turns to read, until I tell you to stop. I really want to see you get into character as you read each part, so that I know what you can do. Bonnie, dear, you go first.'

The play was an extremely dramatic historical one, and normally the fourth formers would have enjoyed reading it enormously. But they could not forgive the new mistress for her harsh treatment of Nora, who was an extremely popular member of the form, and – with the exception of Bonnie, who seemed determined to impress Miss Tallant – they read their parts as sullenly as they dared. After a particularly poor show from Pam, who had read her part in an expressionless monotone, Miss Tallant shook her head, and sighed. 'Dear me! Bonnie seems to be the only member of the form with any dramatic flair at all. It is your turn next.' The mistress pointed at June. 'And for goodness' sake, do try and put a little *expression* into it.'

The corners of June's mouth twitched humorously. So, Miss Tallant wanted her to be expressive, did she? Well, she would give the drama teacher just what she had asked for.

'Do you mind if I stand up, Miss Tallant?' the girl asked politely. 'I feel that I will be able to throw myself into the part more.'

'Very well,' said the mistress. 'But do hurry up, for there are only ten minutes of the lesson left.'

Winking at Freddie, June got to her feet – then what a surprise the class, and Miss Tallant, had. For June really *did* throw herself into the part of the dashing young hero! Putting on a deep, booming voice, she read the lines loudly – so loudly that Mam'zelle Rougier, who was taking a class in the room next door, wondered who on earth could be speaking. The only male teacher in the school was Mr Young, the music master, and that, most certainly, wasn't his voice!

Enjoying herself hugely, June began to add some actions to her performance – clutching at her brow, throwing her arms out, and even, during one particularly moving moment in her speech, falling to her knees.

Miss Tallant stared at her in astonishment, wondering if the girl really meant to be taken seriously, or if she was playing the fool. The fourth formers, of course, were in no doubt at all, feeling laughter bubble up inside them, though they did their best to hide it. It was fortunate for Nora that June's voice completely drowned out her sudden snort of laughter, or she would probably have been given a second punishment!

'June . . .' began Miss Tallant, in her low, calm voice. But it was no use, for June pretended not to hear, and simply carried on with her impassioned speech.

'June!' said the mistress, speaking a little more loudly. 'I really think . . .'

But, to the amusement of the others, the girl ignored Miss Tallant, almost smacking poor Freddie in the face as she flung her arm back, in a dramatic gesture.

'Here, watch out, June!' cried a startled Freddie, moving her chair back a little, while the others were now quite unable to control their mirth.

Felicity and Susan were holding their sides, while tears slid down Pam's cheeks. Nora had stuffed a hanky into her mouth to stifle her giggles, and even the miserable Olive had a smile on her face. Only Sylvia, who did not have much of a sense of humour, did not seem to understand that June was fooling, and looked puzzled rather than amused.

Miss Tallant, however, noticed none of this, for her attention was all on June. Really, the girl was quite dreadful! And it seemed as if she would go on and on, right through the morning break and into the next lesson! Miss Tallant pursed her lips. She hated to raise her voice, or appear that she was losing control in front of her class, but it seemed as if she would have to!

'JUNE!' shouted the mistress and, at last, June stopped, looking round the class as if she had just woken from a dream.

'So sorry, Miss Tallant,' she said. 'I tend to get rather carried away when I'm acting a part. Perhaps next time I can show you how I would tackle a humorous role.'

'Thank you, June,' said the mistress rather frostily. 'I think that you have now given us a quite adequate display of your – er – talents.'

Just then the bell sounded to signal the end of the lesson, and the girls waited expectantly for Miss Tallant to tell them that they could leave. The mistress looked round the class, her eyes going from one girl to another. At last, she said, 'Well, if this form is an example of the standard at Malory Towers, I can see that I am going to have my work cut out. What Miss Hibbert taught you, I simply don't know.'

Of course, this little speech did nothing at all to endear the new teacher to the girls. Not only had she insulted their beloved Malory Towers, but she had found fault with Miss Hibbert. The fourth formers felt what little respect they had for Miss Tallant waning, for they knew that there was a strict rule among the staff that they did not speak against one another in front of the girls.

'Dreadful woman,' said Pam, as the fourth form went

to the cloakroom to fetch their coats. 'I wonder what she has in store for poor old Nora?'

Nora was not with the others, for, of course, she had had to stay behind to learn what her punishment would be. Sylvia was not there either, for she had gone to speak to Matron about something.

'Well, perhaps it will be a lesson to Nora,' said Olive, rather smugly. 'It will do her good to learn that there is one of the mistresses who won't let her get away with anything!'

'Don't tell me that you're a fan of our spiteful Miss Tallant, Olive?' said Susan, looking at the girl rather hard.

'Of course not,' said Olive hastily, turning a little red. 'I'm just pleased that she can see through Nora, that's all.'

'You keep that nasty tongue of yours still,' said Pam, angrily, giving the girl a little push. It was most unusual for the placid, good-natured Pam to lose her temper, but Nora was her best friend and the girl already felt annoyed with Miss Tallant for picking on her, without this spiteful new girl saying beastly things about her as well.

Seeing that Pam was really upset, Felicity gave her arm a squeeze, saying, 'We'll all back Nora up against Miss Tallant, Pam, you know that. And against anyone else who is mean to her as well.'

This last remark was obviously meant for Olive, who scowled at Felicity, before putting on her coat and going outside.

'Mean beast!' said Bonnie, pulling a face, as the door shut behind the new girl. 'What a lot of spite we are going to have to deal with this term, what with Olive *and* that horrid Miss Tallant.'

'Well, you're a fine one to talk!' said June, quite astonished. 'You were sucking up to Miss Tallant no end.'

'Of course I was,' replied Bonnie, calmly. 'Someone has to.'

'Whatever do you mean, Bonnie?' asked Susan.

'People like Miss Tallant always have to have a favourite,' explained Bonnie. And everyone listened intently. Bonnie might be silly in some ways, but she was surprisingly shrewd, and very good at sizing people up.

'She is the kind of person who needs to have someone who thinks that she is wonderful, and will stick up for her. So, I thought that it might as well be me. It might be useful to us, if she thinks that she has someone on her side.'

'Sort of like a spy in the enemy camp, you mean?' said Felicity.

'Exactly!' said Bonnie.

'I think that's a very good idea,' said Freddie, who had been listening thoughtfully. 'I really do. And Bonnie is certainly the right person to carry it off.'

The others murmured their agreement. With her charming manner, innocent air and sweet smile, Bonnie found it quite easy to get people to confide in her. Often far more than they intended to!

'We had better keep this a secret from Olive,' said Felicity. 'I don't trust her, and she might go running to Miss Tallant and tell her the plan, just to stir up trouble for Bonnie.'

'Perhaps we had better not let Sylvia in on it either,' Julie said. 'She *seems* decent enough, but we don't really know her very well.'

'We know that she can't keep her mouth shut!' said Amy, with a haughty toss of her head. 'I don't know which of the two new girls I dislike more – Olive, or that awful Sylvia.'

'Oh, come off your high horse, Amy,' said Lucy. 'Sylvia might be annoying in a lot of ways, but I don't think she's a bad sort.'

'Neither do I, but perhaps we had better not tell her any secrets just yet, just to be on the safe side,' said Susan. 'She's such a chatterbox that she might let something slip out without meaning to.'

The others agreed, and just then the door opened. Nora came into the cloakroom, a very woebegone expression on her face.

'Fifty lines!' she groaned, sinking down on to one of the wooden benches. 'Just for laughing! Honestly, girls, I'm beginning to think that I'm jinxed this term! First Olive takes a dislike to me, and now Miss Tallant. Am I really so horrible?'

The fourth formers crowded round Nora at once, anxious to reassure her.

'It certainly isn't you who is at fault!' cried Julie. 'Miss Tallant is quite the most unpleasant grown-up that I have ever met, while Olive seems to dislike *everyone*! Though, I must say, you and Bonnie do seem to get under her skin more than the rest of us. I can't think why!'

'I told you – it's because she's jealous,' put in Amy. 'She's so unattractive herself that anyone who is pretty simply makes her *green* with envy.'

June gave a crow of laughter. 'Olive-green!' she cried. 'That's a jolly good nickname for her. Next time she makes one of her spiteful remarks about Nora, or Bonnie, or anyone else for that matter, that's what we'll call her!'

The others approved wholeheartedly of this, and even Nora managed a smile. She cheered up even more when the girls told her about Bonnie's plan to suck up to the new mistress.

'I just hope that it pays off,' she said.

'Well, one thing I am absolutely determined about is that we shan't be asking Miss Tallant to help us with our play, or give us any advice at all,' said Susan firmly. 'I don't want her taking any of the credit for our hard work – we shall do it all by ourselves, and we shan't tell her anything about it at all!'

'Hear, hear!' cried the others, and Lucy asked, 'When are we going to have our next meeting, Susan? We're all simply dying to get started.'

'Well, I've looked at a few scripts, and there is one in particular that I think might be just right for us,' said Susan. 'Let's meet in the common-room on Saturday afternoon, and we can make a decision.'

'Good idea,' said Felicity. 'Now, come along, every-one, let's go out and get some fresh air, or our break will be over.'

'I'm looking forward to starting rehearsals for our play,

aren't you?' said June to Freddie, as the two of them followed the others outside.

'Yes, and that's not all I'm looking forward to,' said June, a wicked expression on her face.

Freddie knew that expression well, and, with a grin, she asked, 'What mischief are you plotting now?'

'Well, Freddie, I was just thinking that this is the last term where we will really be able to let ourselves go and have fun at Malory Towers,' answered June. 'Next term we will all have to knuckle down and study for School Cert. And, once we go up into the fifth form, things like tricks and midnight feasts will be out of the question. We shall have to go all serious and dignified, and set a good example to the lower forms.'

'Golly, so we shall!' said Freddie, much struck.

'And that is why I intend to have as much fun as possible *this* term,' said June. 'Are you with me, Freddie?'

'I should say!' said Freddie, her eyes alight with laughter. 'June, it's your birthday in November, isn't it? Wouldn't it be marvellous to celebrate it with a midnight feast?' Then she frowned. 'As long as Susan agrees to it, of course.'

'She will,' said June, confidently. 'Susan might be a bit goody-goody at times, but she's a sport.'

'And just think of the tricks that we can play on Mam'zelle Dupont!' breathed Freddie, looking quite ecstatic.

June laughed, and said, 'Oh, I have quite a few tricks up my sleeve. And Mam'zelle isn't the only one who is going to be on the receiving end! I think that both of our new girls need taking down a peg or two. And as for that beastly Miss Tallant – well, she had better be jolly careful. We're going to have to think up something very special for her.'

'We will,' vowed Freddie. 'She's going to be really sorry that she was so mean to Nora. The Malory Towers mischief makers are out for revenge!'

Olive is annoying

Of course, it wasn't long before Miss Tallant discovered that June's dramatic performance in her class had been a joke – and she felt extremely angry about it. It was Miss Potts, the stern head of North Tower, who set the new mistress straight. The two were in the mistresses' common-room together when Mam'zelle Rougier walked in and cried, 'Miss Tallant! Was there a man in your class this morning?'

'A man?' repeated Miss Tallant, puzzled. 'Of course not, Mam'zelle Rougier. I was taking the fourth form for drama this morning, and there was certainly no man present.'

'But yes, I heard him,' said Mam'zelle Rougier. 'His voice, it was deep and booming, and he talked, and talked, and . . .'

'Ah, that was June,' said Miss Tallant, her brow clearing. 'She was reading the part of the hero, in the play that we are learning. She gave a most extraordinary performance, flinging herself around all over the place and over-acting like nobody's business! It's quite obvious that she considers herself a very talented actress, but I am afraid that she is nothing of the kind! Why, even her friends were laughing at her! June didn't seem to notice, though, and just kept on going. She didn't strike me as terribly bright, I must say!'

Miss Potts looked up sharply from the work she was marking, and said drily, 'I am afraid that you have been taken in. June is very bright indeed, but unfortunately she chooses to use her good brains to amuse the others, rather than on her work. Watch out for her, Miss Tallant, for now that June has succeeded in duping you once, she will certainly try to do so again.'

'Ah yes, she is a bad girl, that June,' said Mam'zelle Rougier, shaking her head. 'A *very* bad girl. When I think of the tricks that she has played on poor, foolish Mam'zelle Dupont! Of course, *I* am not so easy to fool, and June knows that she would be punished most harshly if she tried any of her tricks on me! But you, Miss Tallant, you are young, and not so experienced in the ways of girls as Miss Potts and myself. Be on your guard, for if June thinks that you are weak, she will certainly take advantage of you, and try to make you look stupid – just as she does with Mam'zelle Dupont!'

The new mistress turned scarlet with humiliation. So, that wretched June had duped her! Well, she would very soon come to regret it! As for Mam'zelle Rougier – how dare she couple her, Miss Tallant, with the weak and silly Mam'zelle Dupont?

'I can assure you that June won't find it so easy to take me in again,' said the mistress rather stiffly. 'Nor will any of the others. I fully intend to nip such silliness in the bud.'

Fortunately, the fourth formers were quite unaware of

Miss Tallant's plans as they gathered in the common-room on Saturday to discuss their contribution to the Christmas concert. Once again, Susan was in charge of the meeting, and she sat at the table in the common-room, with a small pile of scripts in front of her.

The fourth formers from the other towers were there too, as it was to be a joint effort, and the common-room seemed very crowded indeed, with girls perched on top of cabinets and on the arms of chairs. Susan began, 'There are several good plays here, but this is the one that I think would be the best, for it is very short and gives us plenty of scope to add a few touches of our own. Felicity has read it as well, and she agrees with me. The play is called *The Christmas Tree Fairy*, and I'd like to read it out to you all now, and see what you think.'

And, in her low, clear voice, Susan began to read the play. The story was quite a simple one, about a fairy doll who has been abandoned in a dusty attic, along with lots of other old toys, and is rescued by a lonely little girl.

'I like it,' said Pam decidedly, as Susan finished her reading. 'It really captures the spirit of Christmas somehow.'

'And I love it when the toys come to life, when there's no one around!' squeaked Bonnie excitedly.

'We won't have to worry about shifting scenery either,' said Felicity. 'For the whole thing takes place in the attic.'

'Yes, but it's far too short,' complained Mary from South Tower. 'It certainly won't fill half an hour.'

'It will by the time we've finished with it,' said Susan.

'We can add a few jokes, and perhaps a song and dance routine. I think it'll be super.'

'Good idea,' said Mary. 'But who is going to write the song?'

'How about you, Mary?' suggested Felicity. 'You're excellent at music.'

'Good idea!' said Susan. 'That's settled, Mary. You are our official songwriter.'

'Oh, my word!' cried Mary, a comical expression of dismay on her face. 'What *have* I let myself in for?'

The others laughed, and Mary's friend Doreen clapped her on the shoulder, crying, 'Don't make a song and dance about it, old girl! I'll help you out.'

'June and Freddie, I have a job for you two as well,' said Susan.

'Us?' chorused the two girls, looking very surprised. 'What do you want us to do, Susan?'

'I want you to take the script away and add a few jokes here and there,' said Susan. 'It's quite a sentimental play, and I think it needs a touch of humour. And who better than the two form jokers to add one!'

Everyone cheered at this, and June and Freddie grinned, both of them absolutely delighted with the task they had been given.

'I'm going to produce the play, with Felicity as my assistant,' said Susan. 'And, of course we will –'

But Susan got no further, for Sylvia called out, 'Susan! If you need anyone else to help produce the play, I am only too keen to help. As you know, I've done this kind of thing before, and you know what they say about many hands making light work.'

'Yes, and I know what they say about too many cooks spoiling the broth,' muttered Susan under her breath to Felicity.

But Felicity was rather touched by the earnest, eager-to-please expression on Sylvia's round, rosy face and she said in a low voice, 'It seems a shame to discourage her when she's so willing. And, who knows, she might prove very useful indeed. Perhaps we should give Sylvia a chance to show what she can do.'

Susan didn't look entirely convinced, but she said, 'Perhaps you're right. But if she becomes too bossy I simply won't stand for it!' Then she raised her voice and said, 'Thank you, Sylvia. A third producer might come in very handy. Now, everyone, I'm going to ask if we can use the big hall for our next meeting, for it really is dreadfully cramped in here. Then we will cast the parts, and decide who is going to help backstage and so on. Any questions?'

There were no questions, but, after the girls from the other three towers had left, there was a good deal of excited chatter. Nora was hoping that she would be considered for the role of the fairy, and said to Pam, 'I do hope that Susan will let me try out for it.'

'Of course she will,' said the loyal Pam, at once. 'You're a marvellous actress, and you can dance beautifully. In fact, I can't think of anyone who could play the fairy as well as you could.'

But someone else was quite certain that *she* was destined to play the role of the fairy – and that someone was Bonnie. 'I have a fairy costume at home that I wore to a fancy-dress party once,' she told Amy, breathlessly. 'I must ask Mother to send it to me.'

'You would certainly make a lovely fairy,' said Amy, looking the pretty, dainty girl over with approval. 'I don't think any other girl in the form would fit the role as perfectly as you.'

Bonnie beamed with pleasure and said, 'Will you be trying out for any of the parts, Amy?'

'No, I don't want to push myself forward,' answered Amy rather piously. 'Let the others have a chance.'

The truth was that Amy wasn't particularly good at drama, dancing or singing, and she was well aware that she didn't stand a chance of getting one of the lead parts. And as she wasn't going to be centre stage, the girl would have preferred not to be involved in the project at all. But this was a vain hope, for Susan wanted everyone to play a part in the success of the form's play, however small.

'Though I can't imagine what we are going to find for Olive to do,' she said to Felicity, as the fourth formers got ready for bed that evening. 'The only talent she seems to have is for rubbing people up the wrong way!'

Felicity laughed and said, 'Well, if all she's going to do is stir things up and cause ill feeling, perhaps it would be best just to leave her out altogether.'

But Susan wouldn't hear of this, and she said stubbornly, 'No, Olive is a member of our form, whether she likes it or not. And she is jolly well going to take part in our play!'

'I wonder why she is so bad-tempered and angry all the time?' said Felicity, with a frown. 'I do hope that she settles down and cheers up a bit, for the sight of her miserable, scowling face puts a damper on everything!'

But, as Pam remarked a few days later, Olive only seemed happy if someone else was getting into trouble.

'She's so spiteful and mean-spirited,' said Pam, with distaste, as the fourth formers got changed after lacrosse practice. 'Did you see the smirk on her face when Miss Maxwell ticked Amy off for not trying hard enough?'

'And she nearly laughed herself sick when June got Mam'zelle Dupont to use that trick pencil in French this morning,' said Nora.

'Well, we *all* laughed at that,' pointed out Julie. 'That was the whole idea, after all!'

'Yes, but Olive wasn't laughing at the joke,' said Nora. 'She was gloating over the tremendous scolding that June got from Mam'zelle afterwards.'

'Good!' said Bonnie, with satisfaction. Then, as the others turned to look at her in surprise, she went on, 'Because June will have it in for Olive, and will get her own back on her. And I, for one, am looking forward to it!'

As Bonnie flounced off with Amy, Susan gave a sigh and said, 'I do so hate all this spite and bad feeling that seems to be brewing.'

'Horrible, isn't it?' agreed Felicity. 'Though I must say, Olive has rather brought it on herself. Petty spite is one of the hardest faults to forgive, and it always stirs up more spite in return.'

'Yes, you're quite right,' said Susan. 'And I think that Bonnie was right, too, when she said that June will try to get her own back on Olive. I say, where *is* June?'

'She and Freddie got changed in a trice, and dashed off somewhere,' said Lucy. 'I wouldn't be a bit surprised if they're plotting revenge on Olive right this very minute.'

'You know, Susan, as head of the form, I really think that it's your duty to speak to Olive about her behaviour,' said Sylvia, an earnest expression on her face.

Susan was rather taken aback, and not at all pleased at this unwanted piece of advice from the new girl. Felicity, too, felt annoyed, and she said, 'Really, Sylvia, I don't think that it's your place –'

But Sylvia didn't even realise that Felicity was speaking, and went on, in her rather loud voice, 'We had a girl just like Olive at my old school. Of course, as head-girl, I had to reprimand her pretty severely. It did the trick, though, if I do say so myself.' She smiled at Susan and said sympathetically, 'There is such a lot to learn when one first becomes head-girl, isn't there? Especially if one has never held a position of responsibility before. But I am always on hand to give help and advice, Susan.'

And, leaving the fourth formers staring after her, open-mouthed, Sylvia put on her coat and went out of the changing room.

Felicity made an explosive little sound of irritation as the door closed behind the new girl, while Susan scoffed,

'As if I would ask Sylvia for advice about anything! If I needed anyone to help me, I would ask you, Felicity, or Pam. You have both had a turn as head-girl, and I'll bet you both made a better job of it than Say-So Sylvia!'

A shout of laughter went up at this, and Nora cried, 'What a marvellous nickname – Say-So Sylvia!'

'I suppose it *is* rather a good nickname,' said Susan, with a pleased grin, and the others chorused, 'IF YOU DO SAY SO YOURSELF!'

June and Freddie, meanwhile, were indeed plotting revenge on Olive. They were up in the dormitory, looking through June's box of tricks, the pair of them chuckling as they recalled jokes that they had played in the past.

'Do you remember the time that Mam'zelle used that soap, which made her face look as if it was streaked with dirt?' laughed Freddie. 'I say! I don't suppose you have any more of it, do you June? That would be a super trick to play on Olive.'

'No, I lent it to my brother, Peter, in the holidays,' answered June, before lapsing into a thoughtful silence. Olive's unpleasant habit of gloating over those who got into trouble rankled with her. Perhaps the girl would think twice about doing it again if *she* was on the receiving end of a scold from one of the mistresses!

June said as much to Freddie, who agreed heartily. 'It would certainly serve her right,' she said. 'I say, can't we think of something to do in Miss Tallant's class tomorrow?

There must be a way that we can get her to lose her temper with Olive.'

June clicked her fingers suddenly. 'I think that there is,' she said, grinning. 'Have you noticed how frightened Olive is of the mice in the biology room?'

'I know that she always sits as far away from their cage as possible,' said Freddie. 'And she jumps every time one of them moves. What have you got in mind, June?'

'Well,' said June, her eyes glinting wickedly. 'Just suppose that one of those mice found its way into Olive's desk. My word, wouldn't she squeal!'

'June!' gasped Freddie. 'It would be a marvellous trick to play, but dare we?'

June, who was bold enough for anything, said at once, 'Of course we dare. Miss Tallant's lesson is right after break, so we can slip along to the biology room at break-time, get one of the mice out and put it into Olive's desk.'

'Poor little mouse,' giggled Freddie. 'Fancy having to face the wrath of Olive! I say, June, he will be able to breathe inside the desk, won't he?'

'Of course,' answered June. 'He won't be in there for long, and I shall return him to his cage as soon as I can.'

'Shall we tell the others?' asked Freddie.

'Yes, let's,' said June. 'But we had better do it when Sylvia is not about. I don't think that they went in much for jokes and tricks at her old school, for, in spite of her jolly, hearty attitude, she doesn't have much of a sense of humour. And we certainly don't want her warning Olive of what's in store for her!'

Freddie nodded and said, 'You're absolutely right about Sylvia. I told her one of my best jokes the other day, and when I had finished she simply looked puzzled. It was quite obvious that she didn't understand it at all. A waste of a perfectly good joke, I thought!'

'Well, when Sylvia has been in the fourth form for a while, perhaps her sense of humour will come to the fore,' said June.

'I don't see how it can fail to,' said Freddie. 'Not once Sylvia realises what fun it is to play tricks and share jokes. That's one of the good things about laughter – it's infectious!'

'Well, one person certainly won't be laughing tomorrow,' said June, with a touch of malice. 'And that will be dear Olive!'

A very successful trick

The fourth formers were in a great state of excitement as they went into Miss Tallant's class the next morning. Everyone but Sylvia – and Olive herself, of course – knew about the trick, and Olive looked puzzled as a few sly glances came her way.

All the mice in the biology room were quite tame, and the one that June had picked up didn't seem to mind being handled at all. He liked it in Olive's desk as well, for there was plenty of room to run around, and lots of interesting things for him to sniff at. 'Quiet, everyone!' hissed Felicity, who was standing by the door. 'Miss Tallant is coming.'

The girls stood up politely as the mistress swept into the room. As usual, she was wearing one of the fussy, frilly blouses that she was so fond of, and a pair of earrings with enormous pink stones in them hung from her ears.

Bonnie, playing up to Miss Tallant for all she was worth, said admiringly, 'Oh, what a lovely blouse, Miss Tallant! You do look so pretty.'

'Why, thank you, Bonnie,' said the mistress, preening a little, while the fourth formers grinned at one another. 'Good morning, girls. Sit down, and we will continue with the play that we began reading the other day. Get your books out, please.'

The fourth formers watched with bated breath as Olive lifted the lid of her desk. But the little white mouse was hiding behind her pencil case, and the girl closed the lid again, without even realising that he was there.

'Never mind,' whispered June to Freddie, Felicity and Susan. 'Olive will have to open her desk again later to put the book away. She's certain to spot the mouse then.'

But the mouse had ideas of his own, and had no intention of waiting until the end of the lesson to make his appearance!

After about ten minutes, he grew rather bored with his new surroundings, and, feeling lonely, decided that he would like to go back to his friends. But how was he to get out? The mouse scuttled into a corner, the sound he made startling Olive very much indeed. What on earth could it be, she wondered? It seemed to be coming from underneath her ink-well. Cautiously, Olive removed the ink-well from its hole in the lid of the desk and the mouse, seeing daylight, stuck his head up through the hole.

Olive's expression of terror was quite comical. For a second she could only sit there, frozen in horror, then she let out a blood-curdling scream, jumping up so hastily that she knocked her chair over.

Miss Tallant, who had been listening intently as Lucy read out part of the play, jumped violently and cried, 'Olive! How dare you disturb the class in this way? Whatever is the matter with you?'

Her eyes wide with horror and her hand trembling, Olive pointed at her desk and stammered, 'A m-mouse! In my d-desk!'

The little mouse had been quite as frightened of Olive as she had been of him, particularly when she screamed so loudly, and he had swiftly retreated back through the hole, into the safety of the desk. He moved so quickly that even Sylvia, who sat next to Olive and turned her head sharply as the girl screamed, hadn't spotted him.

As for Miss Tallant, she didn't quite know what to think. On the one hand, she sincerely hoped that there wasn't a mouse in the desk, for she didn't like them any better than Olive did. But if, on the other hand, there was no mouse, that would mean that Olive was playing a trick, for no other purpose than to disrupt the class.

June, seeing the uncertainty on the mistress's face, was quick to take advantage of it.

'I'll take a look, if you like, Miss Tallant,' she offered, standing up. 'I'm not afraid of mice, and if there is one in Olive's desk I shall be able to remove it.'

The mistress had made up her mind that she didn't like June at all, after learning that her peculiar performance in class the other day had been a joke, but she felt extremely grateful to her now, and said in a relieved tone, 'Thank you, June. Please do so at once.'

June strode up to Olive's desk, saying, 'Better stand aside, Olive, just in case he makes a dash for it. You don't want him running up your leg.'

Olive certainly didn't want that, and she hastily stepped

into the aisle, moving towards the back of the room. June opened the desk, and immediately spotted the poor little mouse, cowering in a corner. Standing with her back to Olive, so that the girl couldn't see what she was doing, she swiftly picked up the tiny creature, slipping it into the deep pocket of her skirt. If only he didn't poke his head out and give the game away! But the mouse, quite worn out by his adventure, rather liked the warmth and softness of June's pocket and decided to settle down there for a nap!

Some of the others had seen what June had done, though, and were now struggling to contain their laughter! This became extremely difficult for them when the wicked June began rummaging violently in Olive's desk for the mouse, scattering books, pencils and all kinds of belongings over the floor. At last she straightened up and, facing Miss Tallant, said solemnly, 'There is most definitely no mouse in Olive's desk.'

'There is!' cried Olive. 'I saw it, I tell you.'

Miss Tallant, feeling bolder now that June had assured her there was no mouse, moved towards Olive's desk and peered in. Of course, there was nothing to be seen, and Miss Tallant pursed her lips, turning to Olive.

'Pick up your belongings from the floor at once,' she said coldly. 'And put them back in your desk.'

The mistress looked and sounded so angry that Olive didn't dare to argue. But as the girl turned away, her eye caught June's and she saw the glint of malice there. Suddenly she realised the truth. June was responsible for the mouse being in her desk. And June must have removed it. But where was the creature now? Olive's eyes fell on the suspicious-looking bulge in June's pocket, and she thought that she saw a slight movement. So that was it, she thought, her eyes narrowing. June had somehow managed to slip the mouse into her pocket. Olive opened her mouth to tell Miss Tallant what had happened, but June hissed, under her breath, 'If you sneak it will be the worse for you.'

She sounded so menacing that Olive felt quite alarmed. Sneaks were not looked upon favourably at any school, she knew that. And there was no point in making her life at Malory Towers any more difficult than it already was. So Olive shut her mouth, said nothing and turned to the task of putting her things back in her desk.

June, meanwhile, went back to her place, winking at the others, who grinned back at her. 'Olive!' snapped Miss Tallant. 'Come and see me when you have finished your lunch.'

'Yes, Miss Tallant,' said Olive bleakly. What a beastly school this was!

'That was simply marvellous, June,' laughed Felicity, as the fourth formers made their way down the corridor after the lesson.

'Yes, and now I had better get this little fellow back to his home,' said June, taking the mouse from her pocket and stroking him with one finger. 'Unless, of course, you want to do it, Olive?'

Olive scowled, then, as June held the mouse out towards her, gave a squeal and ran off down the corridor, the laughter of the fourth formers following her.

'Serves her jolly well right!' said Nora. 'Let's hope that she will think twice before laughing when one of us gets scolded now!'

Sylvia, who had watched in amazement as June produced the mouse from her pocket, said now, 'So there was a mouse, after all! But why did June pretend that she couldn't find it? I don't understand.'

'It was a trick, Sylvia,' explained Pam patiently. 'To pay Olive back for all the times she has crowed over other people when they have got into trouble.'

'Oh,' said Sylvia rather blankly. 'I do hope that June is going to own up to Miss Tallant.'

'Of course she's not, idiot,' said Freddie scornfully. 'The whole idea was to teach Olive a lesson. And that is exactly what we have done!'

'It seems rather mean to me,' said Sylvia, with a frown. 'I really think . . .'

'Sylvia, if you're thinking of sneaking to Miss Tallant, don't!' Susan warned her. 'Because we don't take kindly to sneaks at Malory Towers, and if you aren't careful you might find that *you* become just as unpopular as Olive!'

'I wouldn't dream of sneaking,' said Sylvia stiffly, her rosy complexion turning even redder. 'I just think that June ought to be persuaded to own up. If I were head-girl –'

'Well, you're not,' Felicity interrupted rudely. 'Susan is, and she agrees that Olive needed to be taught a lesson.'

'We *all* agreed,' said Susan, glaring at Sylvia. 'Of course, if you want to go against the whole form, that is quite up to you, Sylvia.'

But Sylvia didn't want to do anything of the sort. She so badly wanted to fit in at Malory Towers and make friends. At once she said, 'Naturally, I shall go along with what the rest of the form decides. I don't like Olive any more than you do, you know, but I think that I would have chosen a different way of dealing with her. I'm not awfully fond of jokes and tricks, you see.'

'How odd!' exclaimed Bonnie. 'That's rather a shame, because we play quite a lot of them in our form. Well, June and Freddie do. Really super ones, too!'

Unsurprisingly, Sylvia didn't look terribly thrilled by this, but as the fourth formers had reached the dining-room by this time, she said no more.

The girl was unusually silent during the meal, lost in her own thoughts. Olive, too, was quiet and sullen, but then she usually was, so the others didn't take much notice of this. As soon as she had finished her meal, Olive left the table and went to find Miss Tallant, to discover what her punishment would be.

'Well, if Miss Tallant gave me fifty lines just for laughing, she's certain to come down much harder on Olive,' said Nora, quite unable to keep the note of glee from her voice.

'After all, she did disrupt the whole class.'

'I think that what Olive did is worth two hundred lines at least,' said Bonnie, happily.

'That ought to keep her busy while we are in the

common-room this evening, so she won't have time to make any of her spiteful remarks!'

But when the fourth formers gathered in the common-room that evening, it seemed that Miss Tallant had not punished Olive at all, for the girl sat down in an armchair and began reading a book.

Felicity nudged Susan and whispered, 'I say, look at Olive. You don't think that she's going to be so silly as to ignore Miss Tallant's punishment, do you?'

Susan frowned at this and, raising her voice, called out, 'Olive! Why aren't you doing the lines that Miss Tallant gave you as a punishment?'

'She didn't give me any lines,' said the girl, sullenly.

'Don't tell me that she let you off scot-free!' exclaimed Pam.

'Olive, you had better not have sneaked on me,' said June sternly. 'I warned you what would happen if you did.'

'I haven't sneaked on you,' retorted Olive, glaring at June. 'But Miss Tallant has given me another punishment, instead of lines.'

'What is it?' asked Felicity. 'Are you to go to bed early?'

'No, I'm to do extra prep with Miss Tallant on Saturday morning,' said Olive gloomily. 'Not that it's any of your business!'

This really was a horrid punishment, for the girls enjoyed having their weekends all to themselves. They were happy, jolly times where everyone could do as they pleased, whether they chose to play games, go horse-riding or simply sit around laughing and joking in the common-room. And next Saturday would be even more fun than usual, for the casting of the Christmas play was to take place that afternoon. But nobody felt in the slightest bit sorry for Olive, for all of the fourth formers thought that she had well and truly earned her punishment.

The girl ignored the grins of the fourth formers and went back to her book, though Felicity, who stole several glances at her, noticed that she didn't turn the pages at all. She's only pretending to be engrossed in her book, thought Felicity. I wonder what is going on in Olive's head? What a odd girl she is!

Most of the fourth formers were looking forward to the meeting on Saturday afternoon, and the rest of the week seemed to pass by very slowly indeed!

But, at last, it was Saturday, and June, looking out of the common-room window after breakfast, said, 'It looks quite sunny for the time of year. Freddie, shall we take a walk along the cliffs in a little while?'

'That would be super,' answered Freddie. 'Would anyone else like to come?'

Amy and Bonnie, neither of whom cared for exercise and fresh air, both shook their heads, but several of the others agreed eagerly to the suggestion.

'Lucy and I will join you,' said Julie. 'But, of course, we will be on horseback.'

'What about you, Olive?' asked June, in a deceptively sweet tone. 'Would you like to come with us? Oh no, half a minute! I completely forgot – you have to do extra prep for Miss Tallant, don't you?'

Everyone laughed, and Olive scowled, before stalking angrily to the door and flouncing out. As the door slammed behind her, Felicity said, 'Miss Tallant will keep her nose to the grindstone, all right, while we are all out enjoying the fresh air.'

'It seems a jolly odd punishment to me, though,' said Bonnie, who had been looking thoughtful. 'I know that Miss Tallant is not on duty this weekend, for she told me so herself. Yet she has chosen to give up part of her Saturday too, so that she can sit in the classroom with Olive.'

This seemed very strange indeed, for the girls knew how hard the mistresses worked, and how they treasured their free time.

'I never thought of that!' exclaimed Lucy. 'Fancy wanting to give up part of a weekend off to spend time with a sourpuss like Olive.'

'Perhaps Miss Tallant has nothing better to do,' said June. 'The mistresses sometimes go home to visit their family or friends when they have a weekend off. Miss Tallant might not have a family. And I'm quite sure that she can't have any friends. I don't think she's awfully popular with the mistresses here either.'

'She's not,' piped up Bonnie. 'I stayed behind to help her tidy the classroom the other day, and she told me that Mam'zelle Dupont dislikes her. So does Miss Potts.'

'She really shouldn't say such things to you, Bonnie,' said Susan disapprovingly. 'I'm quite sure that none of the other mistresses would!'

'I think it's a jolly good thing that she did,' said June

warmly. 'After all, the whole point of Bonnie sucking up to Miss Tallant was so that she could get to know things about her. Well done, Bonnie!'

Of course, this was the first that Sylvia had heard about Bonnie's plan to become Miss Tallant's favourite, and she looked extremely startled.

Seeing her expression, Freddie said, 'I suppose you don't approve, Sylvia?'

'You're wrong,' said Sylvia, to everyone's surprise. 'I don't like Miss Tallant. She's sly, and if Bonnie can find out what she's up to that will be a very good thing.'

Bonnie smiled, and said, 'Actually, it's rather lucky for us that she doesn't seem to have any friends, for that means that I am the only person she has to talk to.'

'I don't think it's lucky at all,' said Nora, dismayed. 'If Miss Tallant is going to start dishing out Saturday morning preps as punishment simply because she has nothing better to occupy her time, we shall all have to watch our step!'

'Golly, yes,' said Julie, horrified. 'I always spend Saturdays with Jack, and Lucy with Sandy. And I'm not very good at English or Drama, so I'm certain to get a row from Miss Tallant sooner or later.'

'Well, perhaps we had better give our dear Miss Tallant something to do,' said June thoughtfully.

'Do you have anything in mind?' asked Felicity.

'Not yet,' said June. 'But I'll think of something, you may be sure. Now, let's go and get our hats and coats on and enjoy the sunshine.'

Miss Tallant interferes

The fourth formers enjoyed their lunch, for their walk in the fresh air had made them very hungry indeed. Only Olive seemed to have no appetite, pushing the food around her plate with a fork, but eating very little. She looked even more miserable than usual, thought Felicity. Miss Tallant had probably given her a really bad time. Despite her dislike of Olive, Felicity couldn't help feeling a little sorry for her, and said kindly, 'You must feel glad that your punishment is over, Olive. Did Miss Tallant give you a lot of extra work to do?'

'Quite a lot,' answered Olive, who was surprised to discover that she felt a little cheered by Felicity's interest. Then Bonnie, who was sitting nearby, said, 'Well, I walked by the classroom earlier, and you certainly didn't seem to be working very hard then. You were standing by Miss Tallant's desk, and the two of you were talking about something.'

'She was explaining the work to me,' snapped Olive, giving Bonnie a look of dislike. 'And how dare you spy on me?'

'I wasn't spying,' said Bonnie, with a disdainful little laugh. 'I just happened to be passing. As if I would want to spy on *you*.'

Olive flushed angrily, and lapsed into her usual morose silence. When the meal was over and the girls left the dining-room, Olive turned to go towards the common-room. Susan called her name, and said, 'Where do you think you're going? Have you forgotten that we are holding auditions for our play in the hall?'

Olive hadn't forgotten, for the girls had talked of little else for days. But she had been hoping to slip away unnoticed, and avoid having anything to do with the stupid play.

'Do I have to come?' she asked Susan now, her mouth set in a discontented droop.

'Yes, you jolly well do,' answered Susan sternly. 'Just for once, Olive, show a bit of team spirit, and do something to help the form.'

So, reluctantly, Olive followed the others over to the big hall. There was a stage at one end of the room, with several rows of chairs set out in front of it. Felicity, Susan and Sylvia, as producers, took three chairs in the front row, while the rest of the fourth form filed into the seats behind. There was a great deal of scraping of chairs and shuffling of feet, but once the noise died down, Susan stood up and addressed everyone. 'Well, girls, you all know why we are here,' she said in her clear voice. 'So let's begin casting the parts, and not waste any time. Of course, the two most important roles in the play are those of the fairy doll, and Amelia, the little girl who finds her. Now, who is interested in auditioning for the part of the fairy?'

Three girls put their hands up at once. One was Jenny,

a tall, dark, West Tower girl, who had a beautiful singing voice. The second was Nora. And the third, of course, was Bonnie.

'Very well, we shall try all three of you out in the part,' said Susan. 'As you know, whoever plays the fairy has to sing and dance, as well as act, so we really need someone who is a good all-rounder. Jenny, if you would like to take the stage first, please, we can –'

Just then the big door at the back of the hall opened, and Susan stared in surprise as Miss Tallant entered. The rest of the girls turned to see who had come in, getting politely to their feet when they realised that it was one of the mistresses. But whatever was she doing here?

They soon found out! Miss Tallant strode briskly to the front of the hall and said, 'Sit down, please, Susan.'

Astonished, and none too pleased, Susan did as she was told, and Miss Tallant faced the fourth formers.

'I understand that you have decided to perform a play called *The Christmas Tree Fairy*,' she said. 'Quite a good little play, though rather short.'

The fourth formers looked at one another in consternation. This was *their* play. What business of Miss Tallant's was it? Susan spoke up. 'We are going to make it longer by adding a few touches of our own, Miss Tallant.'

'I see,' said the mistress. 'What do you have in mind?'

'Well, we are going to add a song and dance, and June and Freddie are going to write a few jokes,' explained Susan.

Miss Tallant gave a cold little smile and said, 'Indeed?

Well, I shall have to approve them first. Now, I suggest that we begin casting the parts.'

The girls began to mutter among themselves, quite horrified now. Miss Tallant was trying to take over their play!

Susan, however, had other ideas. As head of the form, it was up to her to take the lead and she stood up and faced the mistress. This was really very brave of Susan, for she knew that Miss Tallant could be spiteful and vindictive, and her knees shook a little. But her voice was steady as she said firmly, 'Excuse me, Miss Tallant. I don't mean to be rude, but Felicity, Sylvia and I are going to produce the play, and the three of us would like to decide who to cast in the different parts.'

Miss Tallant stared at Susan as if she was something extremely nasty, and said coldly, 'And just what do you girls know about producing a play?'

June, whose temper had been rising as she listened to the mistress, got to her feet and said, 'Nothing at all, Miss Tallant. And we won't have the chance to learn anything if we aren't left alone to make our own mistakes.'

Miss Tallant turned quite white with anger and hissed, 'How dare you cheek me like that, June? I should watch your step, if I were you, or I might feel compelled to enquire a little more closely into that affair of the mouse in Olive's desk.'

June blinked, quite lost for words, for once. How on earth had Miss Tallant come to suspect that she, June, was behind that? Suddenly, yet another interruption occurred.

Miss Williams, the fourth-form mistress, had seen Miss

Tallant go into the hall, and had frowned to herself. She knew very well that her form was holding a meeting about the play, and wondered what Miss Tallant was doing there. Only that morning, Miss Williams had spoken to Susan about the play, and the girl had said politely, but very decidedly, that the fourth formers wanted to do everything themselves, without asking for any assistance from Miss Tallant. Miss Williams had been pleased to hear this, for it would be a very good thing for the girls to take responsibility for their play, and learn how to organise themselves. Moreover, the fourth-form mistress did not like Miss Tallant, and she felt that the new mistress might well be more of a hindrance than a help to the girls. Miss Williams went across to the door of the big hall and pushed it open a crack, so she heard what Miss Tallant said to Susan. She had been about to intervene herself when she heard the way that Susan coolly stood up to the mistress, and she smiled to herself. Then June spoke, and Miss Williams, opening the door a little wider, saw the angry, spiteful look on Miss Tallant's face. The trouble with June was that she was likely to get carried away, and perhaps go too far in her rebellion against Miss Tallant. And then the girl would only end up getting herself into trouble.

So Miss Williams strode briskly into the room and said, 'I am sorry to interrupt your meeting, but . . . Why, Miss Tallant, what are you doing here? Susan, I distinctly remember you telling me that you intended to produce the play yourself, with assistance from Felicity and Sylvia.

And I must say that I was very pleased to hear it. Don't tell me that you have changed your minds?'

'No, Miss Williams,' said Susan, noticing a glint in Miss Williams's eye and realising that the mistress was well aware of what had been happening. 'Miss Tallant very kindly offered her services, but I was just telling her that there was no need for her to trouble herself over us.'

'Most commendable!' said Miss Williams warmly. 'It's always nice to see you girls using your initiative and doing things for yourselves. Miss Tallant and I shan't hold you up any longer.' Then she turned to the other mistress, and said brightly, 'Come along, Miss Tallant. The girls are very busy, so let's leave them to it.'

Miss Tallant had no choice but to follow Miss Williams from the hall. And once the door had closed behind the two mistresses, a perfect hubbub broke out.

'Of all the nerve!'

'Who does Miss Tallant think she is? How dare she try to order us about like that?'

'Thank heavens that Miss Williams turned up when she did.'

'Yes, she has sized Miss Tallant up, all right,' said Susan. 'And now that they have both gone, let's get down to business!'

So, one by one, Jennifer, Bonnie and Nora took to the stage, as the rest of the fourth form watched with interest.

Jennifer's singing was so lovely that the fourth formers cheered when she came to the end of her song. She read a few lines from the play, too, and Felicity murmured to

Susan and Sylvia, 'She's not a bad actress. A little stiff, perhaps, but I daresay that's because she feels nervous.'

Then Mary sat down at the piano and played a lively tune, while Jennifer danced. Alas, her dancing was nowhere near as good as her singing or her acting, and Sylvia said, 'Well, I suppose it would be too much to expect her to be good at everything.'

'That's just it, though,' said Susan. 'The girl who takes this part *has* to be good at everything.' Then she raised her voice and said, 'Thank you, Jennifer, you may sit down now. Bonnie! Your turn next.'

There was no doubt that little Bonnie certainly looked the part of the fairy to perfection. She seemed even smaller and daintier than usual as she stood alone on the big stage. She danced gracefully and, when it came to reading the lines, the girl really threw herself into the part. Alas, Bonnie floundered when it came to the song, for not only was she out of tune, her voice was so high pitched that some of the listening girls covered their ears. Grimacing, Susan said, 'Simply awful! A pity, because she acts and dances well.'

Then it was Nora's turn. Nora's singing voice was not as pure as Jennifer's, but it was very pleasant, and the fourth formers clapped eagerly when she finished her song. And she was by far the best dancer of the three girls. Nora proved, too, that she was a fine little actress, and Felicity said, 'Nora is very humorous, too, and I feel quite sure that she will be excellent at doing the jokes and the funny lines that June and Freddie are going to write.'

Susan and Sylvia agreed with this at once, and Susan said happily, 'Well, it looks as if we have found our fairy! I shan't tell Nora yet, though. We shall audition for the other parts first, and let everyone know what we have decided at the end.'

'Bonnie isn't going to be too pleased,' said Felicity. 'I just hope that she doesn't throw a tantrum. You know how difficult she can be if things don't go her way.'

'Don't you worry about Bonnie, Felicity,' said Susan firmly. 'I shall deal with her when the time comes.'

Felicity felt a little apprehensive. Susan had a blunt way of speaking at times, and didn't always see that it was sometimes necessary to handle things with a little tact.

The auditions went very smoothly indeed, and both Felicity and Susan found themselves warming to Sylvia. The girl hadn't tried to push herself forward at all, and had worked amicably alongside Felicity and Susan. Soon all of the parts had been cast, and it was time to let the fourth formers in on the decisions that had been reached.

Susan stood up to face the girls, and said, 'Thank you to all of you who auditioned. Everyone did very well indeed. And now it's time to tell you who is going to play each part.'

The listening girls sat in expectant silence, those who had auditioned feeling both nervous and excited. At last Susan said, 'We have decided that the lead role of the fairy doll will be given to . . . Nora!'

A great cheer went up at this, while Nora looked as if she simply couldn't believe her ears. Those closest to the girl clapped her on the back, and Pam cried, 'Splendid choice! You'll be marvellous, Nora, old girl.'

Jennifer managed to hide her disappointment, and congratulated Nora, but Bonnie was quite unable to hide hers. Her bottom lip jutted out, and she scowled fiercely at Susan.

'Horrid beast!' she lisped to Amy. 'Susan has never liked me, because I used to be friends with Felicity, and this is her way of getting back at me. I don't like Miss Tallant, but perhaps it would have been a good thing if she had stayed after all, for I'm sure that *she* would have chosen me for the part.'

Once the noise and excitement had died down, Susan announced, 'Amelia, the little girl, is to be played by Molly.'

Molly, a very small girl from East Tower, with rather a serious expression, suddenly found herself beaming from ear to ear, as a rousing 'hurrah!' went up from the East Tower girls.

Quickly Susan gave out the other parts. Pam was to play Amelia's aunt, Julie was going to be a toy soldier, and Lucy laughed out loud when she learned that she was to dress up in a big, furry costume and play a teddy bear!

'There will be something for everyone to do,' said Susan. 'Mary is writing a song for us, of course, while June and Freddie are adding some humorous touches to the script. And we're going to need plenty of people to help paint scenery and do hair and make-up, and so on.'

'I've a good mind not to do anything at all to help,' muttered a disgruntled Bonnie to Amy.

But Susan hadn't finished. 'There is one more thing,' she said. 'There is one person I haven't mentioned, who is going to be very important to our little play. In fact, I would go so far as to say that she is vital.'

The fourth formers looked at one another in surprise. Who on earth could Susan be talking about?

'That person is our wardrobe mistress,' said Susan, looking very serious indeed.

'Because there are so many costumes, we really need someone who is an expert at needlework. Someone who has flair and taste, and a good eye for detail. Someone who, once she sets her mind to a task, works tirelessly to complete it. There is only one person in the form – in the whole *school*, in fact – who fits that description. And that person is Bonnie Meadows.'

Bonnie gave a gasp, her big brown eyes growing even bigger. Instantly, her disappointment at not being cast as the fairy was forgotten. And Susan was no longer a mean beast. On the contrary, she was very shrewd and perceptive indeed. Bonnie couldn't imagine how she had ever thought that she didn't like her!

Felicity grinned to herself. Good old Susan! She was learning that, with some people, a little tact worked wonders. Now she had turned Bonnie's sulks to smiles, and made sure that the fourth formers had an excellent wardrobe mistress, in the neatest possible way! Most of the others guessed what Susan was up to as well, and played along by cheering Bonnie, and praising her extravagantly.

'Simply marvellous! I can't think of anyone who would do a better job!'

'Yes, we can be sure of having just the right costumes now, with old Bonnie in charge.'

'I should say! Good for you, Bonnie!'

Bonnie beamed round and thanked everyone prettily. 'I shan't let you down,' she said. 'And I shall be glad of some help from anyone who is good with a needle, for there will be a lot of work to do.'

Several girls from other towers immediately volunteered their services, and Bonnie said, 'Perhaps tomorrow afternoon we can all go and look in that little room behind the stage, where all the old costumes from past Malory Towers plays are stored. We are sure to find some things that will be useful to us in there.'

'My word, you're eager, Bonnie,' called out Julie.

'If a job's worth doing, it's worth doing well,' said Bonnie, briskly. 'I intend to take my responsibility as wardrobe mistress very seriously indeed. Now, if you'll excuse me, the library has a fine book on play costumes, so I think I shall pop along there and borrow it.' Then she called out to the girls who had offered to help her, 'Two o'clock sharp, tomorrow afternoon, you girls.'

And with that, she walked purposefully from the room, as Felicity chuckled, 'Bonnie really *does* go all out when she takes on a task. I feel quite sorry for the girls who have offered to help her, for I think that she may turn out to be quite a slave-driver!'

Susan laughed at that, and said, 'Well, I call that a

highly successful meeting – in spite of Miss Tallant's attempts to sabotage it! Mary told me that she has almost finished writing the song, and June and Freddie have already written a few jokes into the script – and very funny they are, too. At this rate, it won't be long before we are able to hold our first rehearsal. Shall we go back to the common-room before tea?'

Felicity agreed to this at once, and as the two girls were walking along the corridor, June and Freddie caught them up. June's expression was unusually serious, and Felicity asked, 'Anything up, old girl?'

'Yes, there is, actually,' said June. 'It has just occurred to me that Miss Tallant knew the name of the play we are doing. But how *could* she know, for we haven't told anyone outside the form. And we agreed that we weren't going to tell Miss Tallant anything.'

'Perhaps someone let something slip out by accident,' suggested Susan.

'Who would do *that*?' asked Freddie rather scornfully. 'It's not as if any of us are in the habit of having cosy chats with Miss Tallant, for none of us can bear her.'

June's brow cleared suddenly, and she snapped her fingers. 'Bonnie!' she cried. 'She's always hanging round Miss Tallant, offering to help tidy the classroom and what-not.'

'Yes, but only as part of her plan to suck up to her,' Felicity reminded June. 'She certainly doesn't do it because she has any real liking for Miss Tallant.'

'I know that,' said June. 'But she could easily have

83

given something away by accident. And there's something else, too. Miss Tallant mentioned that business with the mouse, and it was pretty clear that she suspected I was involved. I don't see how she can have reached that conclusion unless someone told her.'

'Yes, we all heard her say that,' said Susan, looking grave. 'I didn't think anything of it at the time, but you're quite right, of course. We certainly don't want our dear Miss Tallant poking her nose into fourth-form business.'

The others were in wholehearted agreement with this, and June said, 'Bonnie said that she was going to the library, didn't she? Well, let's find her and tackle her about it. She has to learn that it simply isn't on to give away fourth-form secrets!'

Bonnie in trouble

June stormed off down the corridor, the other three in hot pursuit. Susan caught up with her as they reached the library, and grabbed her arm.

'Now look here, June,' she began. 'Don't go rushing in and accusing Bonnie of things, when, for all we know, she may be quite innocent.'

'Susan is quite right,' said Felicity. 'I know that Bonnie can be devious in some ways, but I really don't think . . .'

Her voice tailed off suddenly, for through the glass pane in the library door, Felicity had spotted Bonnie sitting at a table with a book. And bending over to speak to her, her blonde head very close to Bonnie's darker one, was Miss Tallant. Both of them were smiling, and Miss Tallant patted Bonnie's shoulder, before reaching into her bag and pulling out a bar of chocolate. She handed this to Bonnie, then walked towards the door. Swiftly, the four girls outside retreated along the corridor before they were spotted, and went into one of the empty music-rooms.

'Well!' said Freddie, looking astonished. 'Did you see that?'

The other three nodded, and June said grimly, 'Well, that seems to point to Bonnie being the culprit. And from the look of things, the information she passed to Miss Tallant certainly didn't slip out by accident.'

June felt just as shocked and dismayed as the others, for although she had suspected Bonnie, she had never, for one second, imagined that the girl's actions had been deliberate.

'It certainly looks that way,' said Susan, frowning deeply. 'Why would Miss Tallant have given Bonnie chocolate, unless it was in return for a favour?'

No one could imagine, and Felicity said thoughtfully, 'This puts a different complexion on things. If Bonnie *is* sneaking fourth-form secrets to Miss Tallant, it might be best not to tackle her just yet, for it will put her on her guard.'

'Quite right,' said June. 'Until we can think of a way of catching Bonnie out, we must carry on as usual, and all behave in a perfectly normal way towards her.'

'What do you think, Susan?' asked Freddie. 'You are head of the form, after all.'

'Yes, I agree with Felicity and June,' said Susan, who was looking very upset indeed. 'I must say that I am terribly disappointed in Bonnie. I know that she and I have had our differences, but I really didn't think that she would stoop this low.'

'Shall we tell the others?' asked Felicity.

Susan thought for a moment, then said, 'No. Obviously we can't say anything in front of Amy, for she is Bonnie's friend. We can't rely on Sylvia to keep her mouth shut either, and as for Olive – well, I certainly don't trust *her*!'

All the same, the four girls found it very difficult to stick to their word and behave normally with Bonnie. They had very strict ideas of honour, and anyone who sneaked, or gave away secrets, was beneath contempt, as far as they were concerned. It was June who came up with an idea to trap Bonnie, a few days later. She and Freddie got into a huddle with Felicity and Susan in the courtyard one break-time.

'We will pretend that we are planning to play a trick on Miss Tallant, and make sure that Bonnie overhears us,' explained June. 'Then Bonnie will run off and tell her tales, and Miss Tallant will try to foil our trick.'

'And that will prove that Bonnie is working against the fourth form,' said Felicity with a sigh. 'What do you have in mind, June?'

'Well, I thought we could pretend that we are going to do something similar to the mouse trick that we played on Olive,' answered June. 'We could say that we are going to put a big spider in the drawer of Miss Tallant's desk, perhaps.'

'Good idea,' said Freddie. 'Miss Tallant is very like Mam'zelle Dupont in that she doesn't care for spiders, or mice or anything like that.'

'Exactly!' said June. 'We will make sure that Bonnie is nearby when we are plotting, and we shall be able to judge from Miss Tallant's reaction when she goes to her desk whether Bonnie has sneaked.'

'Very well,' said Susan. 'The sooner we get definite proof that Bonnie is the one giving things away to Miss Tallant, the better, I suppose.'

So when the four girls went into the common-room that evening, they made a point of sitting close to Bonnie. The girl had her head bent over her needlework, as usual, and was chattering away to Amy as she sewed. Pam, Sylvia and Olive were there as well, while the others had gone off to see a slide show in the big hall.

'I simply can't wait to see Miss Tallant's face when she opens her drawer tomorrow and that spider runs towards her,' said June, in rather a loud voice.

Freddie giggled. 'We're going to find a spider in the gardener's shed,' she said. 'A big, fat one, with thick, hairy legs.'

'Ugh!' said Susan, giving a shudder. 'I can't say that I'm awfully keen on spiders myself. It will be funny to see how Miss Tallant reacts, though. And it will jolly well serve her right for trying to spoil our meeting the other day.'

'When are you going to play the trick?' asked Felicity. 'Monday morning? Jolly good.'

The four moved away then, to join Pam, who raised her eyebrows and said, 'What's this? Hatching a plot?'

The four girls looked at one another, and Susan said, 'Shall we tell Pam our secret? Let's, for we know we can trust her.'

Quickly, June explained that they suspected Bonnie of telling tales to Miss Tallant, and of their plan to catch her out.

Pam listened intently, her expression very serious. At last, she said, 'I simply can't believe that Bonnie is on Miss Tallant's side.'

'None of us wants to believe it, Pam,' said Felicity, earnestly. 'I know that Bonnie has some funny ways, but I honestly believed that she was completely straight. But if you had seen her in the library with Miss Tallant, you would agree that her behaviour was most suspicious.'

'Hush!' hissed Freddie. 'She's coming over.'

Bonnie joined them, saying excitedly, 'Susan, I have some super ideas for costumes. I've made some sketches and must show them to you.'

'I'm looking forward to seeing them,' said Susan, forcing herself to smile at the girl. 'Bring them to me tomorrow, if you like.'

'I will,' said Bonnie. 'I say, did I hear you talking about playing a trick on that horrid Miss Tallant.'

'Yes,' said June, winking slyly at the others. 'We are going to put a huge spider in her desk on Monday, but you must promise to keep it to yourself.'

'Of course,' said Bonnie, clapping her hands together in excitement. 'I shan't say a word. Oh, how I shall enjoy hearing her squeal!'

With that Bonnie went back to join Amy, and Freddie said, 'See! Even more proof, if we needed it. What a nerve, coming over like that to try and get more information out of us.'

Pam looked thoughtful, and said, 'I must say, she's a jolly convincing actress.'

'Well, we'll see how convincing she is when she's been well and truly caught out,' said June, in a hard voice. 'And then we will decide how to punish her.'

All of those who were in on the secret were looking forward to Miss Tallant's Drama class on Monday. As usual, Bonnie held the door open for the mistress, receiving a warm smile and a word of praise. June, who was watching Miss Tallant closely, thought that there was a triumphant glint in the mistress's eye as she walked towards her desk. She didn't go right up to it, though, noticed June, but stopped a few feet away from it – almost as if she was afraid that there was something unpleasant in there.

'Sit down girls,' she said. The girls did as they were told and, for a moment, the mistress stood watching them, her eyes hard and cold. They seemed to linger on June, and, at last, she said, 'June, please come out to the front of the class.'

June stood up, her head bowed so that the mistress would not see the little smile on her lips, and walked to the front of the room. Miss Tallant looked her up and down coldly, then said, 'Please open the drawer of my desk.'

June put on a puzzled look, and said, 'Open your drawer, Miss Tallant? But why?'

'Don't ask questions, June,' said the mistress. 'Just do as you are told.'

So June pulled open the drawer, noticing as she did so that Miss Tallant shrank back a little. Then the mistress peered over June's shoulder and said, 'Now kindly remove the spider that is lurking in there.'

'Spider? What spider?' said June, looking so puzzled, and so innocent, that Felicity had to clamp her lips tightly together to stop her laughter escaping.

'The spider that I know very well you have hidden

there,' said Miss Tallant, a triumphant note in her voice.

'Miss Tallant, I would never do such a thing!' said June, sounding so outraged that Freddie grinned. 'Why, the very thought of playing a trick on a mistress is –'

'June, your reputation for playing tricks and jokes on mistresses is well known to me,' interrupted Miss Tallant. 'So please don't waste your breath. I know that you have put a spider in that drawer, and I insist that you remove it immediately. After you have done so, I shall inform you what your punishment is to be.'

'But Miss Tallant, there is no spider there,' said June, looking down into the drawer. 'See for yourself.'

Rather gingerly, Miss Tallant looked. 'It must be hiding in one of the corners. Remove everything from the drawer, June, and put it on top of the desk.'

Obediently, June did so, then at last she stood back and said, 'There is no spider there, Miss Tallant.'

Miss Tallant was reluctantly forced to agree that there wasn't, and she said crossly, 'I believe that you have hidden it, just as you did the mouse. Turn out your pockets, at once.'

June turned out her pockets but, of course, there was no spider, and she said cheekily, 'You're quite welcome to feel in them yourself, Miss Tallant, if you think that I am hiding anything else.'

But Miss Tallant had no intention at all of doing this. If she did find a spider in June's pocket, she would simply die! Yet she couldn't let this wretched girl get the better of her.

Miss Tallant had been reliably informed that June intended to put a spider in her drawer today, and she was going to punish her for it.

'June, you will go to bed one hour early tonight,' said the mistress spitefully, and the fourth formers gasped in outrage.

'You can't punish June without any evidence!' cried Susan, stung by the injustice of this, and Miss Tallant glared at her.

'I can do anything I please,' she said in an icy tone, before turning back to June. 'Put your belongings back in your pocket,' she said. 'Then go back to your seat and we will get on with the lesson.'

Susan opened her mouth to protest again, but Felicity whispered, 'Don't, Susan. You will only earn a punishment for yourself. We are going to have to think of some other way to defeat Miss Tallant.'

So, reluctantly, Susan remained silent.

June, meanwhile, stole a glance at Bonnie's face as she made her way back to her seat. The girl really *was* a good actress, for she looked just as shocked as everyone else. June made up her mind that she was going to tackle her later over her deceit – and, my goodness, wouldn't she give her something to look shocked about! The girl wasn't terribly upset about her punishment, though having to go to bed early was a frightful bore. But she *was* upset by the fact that the punishment was an unjust one. She intended to use her hour of peace and quiet to good purpose, however – in thinking up a way to get back at Miss Tallant!

'Phew!' said Pam, when the girls emerged from the classroom. 'What a lesson! How I dislike that woman.'

'It's so terribly unfair!' cried Susan. 'June is being punished for something that she hasn't even done.'

'Don't worry about me, Susan,' said June. 'The main thing is that it proved our suspicions are correct, and that Bonnie is giving our secrets away to Miss Tallant. Where *is* Bonnie, anyway?'

'Oh, she stayed behind to help Miss Tallant tidy up the classroom,' said Nora. 'But what's all this about Bonnie telling her our secrets?'

'Of course, you don't know, do you?' said Felicity. And she and Susan told Nora, Julie and Lucy what had been happening.

They were very shocked, of course, and Lucy said gravely, 'What are we going to do about it?'

'Speak to her about it, of course,' said June. 'And I vote we punish the little beast by sending her to Coventry.'

'That will be a very hard punishment for her to bear, because Bonnie loves to chatter,' said Julie.

'I wonder if Amy will stand out against the punishment?' said Nora. 'After all, Bonnie is her friend.'

'Well, if she does, then I'm afraid we shall have to send Amy to Coventry, too,' said Susan, her expression grim. 'We'll tackle her in the common-room after tea tonight.'

So, after tea that night, the girls gathered in the common-room.

Susan was sitting with Felicity, Pam and a few others, and she said, 'Well, I vote that we get this whole beastly business over with as quickly as possible.'

The others agreed, and Susan called out, 'Bonnie, can you come over here a minute, please? There is something we need to talk to you about.'

Surprised, Bonnie went over to Susan, who decided that it was no use beating about the bush, and said, 'Bonnie, I need to ask you something. Have you been letting Miss Tallant in on some of our form's secrets?'

Bonnie gave a gasp, and said at once, 'Of course not! What makes you ask such a thing, Susan?'

'She's fibbing!' said June. 'There's no one who can play innocent as well as Bonnie can. And we all know how good she is at acting.'

'That's enough, June,' said Susan sharply. 'The thing is, Bonnie, someone told Miss Tallant the name of the play that we are doing.'

'And they sneaked to her about the mouse that I put in Olive's desk,' said June, who was far too angry to stay silent. 'And we saw her with you in the library on the day of our meeting. She gave you a bar of chocolate.'

'Yes, because she had asked me to do something for her, and said that she would give me a bar of chocolate if I did,' said Bonnie, who had turned pale. 'It was all part of my plan to suck up to her.'

Freddie gave a harsh laugh. 'Yes, but you went a little too far in your plan, didn't you? You decided that you had more to gain from being on Miss Tallant's side than ours.'

'That's a horrid lie!' cried Bonnie, tears starting to her big, brown eyes.

'Of course it is,' said Amy, entering the battle. 'How dare you accuse Bonnie of such a thing?'

'I realise that you want to stick up for your friend, Amy,' said Felicity. 'But we know that Bonnie is the culprit. You see, we let her overhear us talking about June's plan to put a spider in Miss Tallant's desk. And, sure enough, word reached Miss Tallant's ears.'

'But it wasn't me!' protested Bonnie, tears beginning to trickle down her cheeks now. 'I wasn't the only one who overheard you. Sylvia was there that night, and so was Olive. And Pam! It could just as easily have been one of them.'

Of course, the others knew that it wasn't Pam, for she had come up through the school with them and would never dream of such a thing. Felicity couldn't help glancing at Sylvia and Olive, though. Sylvia was looking extremely startled, while Olive wore her usual miserable expression. *Could* it have been one of them? She said to Bonnie, 'All right then, you tell us what this mysterious job was that Miss Tallant asked you to do. Then, perhaps, we will believe you.'

But Bonnie had a stubborn streak, and she pursed her lips, saying through her tears, 'I shan't tell you, for if you were true friends you would believe me, and wouldn't expect me to explain myself to you like this.'

'So you are refusing to tell us?' said Susan, looking grave.

Bonnie's soft, brown curls shook as she nodded her head.

'Don't be an ass, Bonnie!' begged Felicity. 'Just tell us what Miss Tallant wanted you to do, and that will be an end to all of this.'

This time Bonnie shook her head, a stubborn set to her firm little chin.

'Then I am afraid, Bonnie, that we will have to assume that you are the sneak,' said Susan heavily. 'And your punishment is that you will be sent to Coventry. Not one girl in the form is to talk to you, or have anything to do with you, for a whole week.'

Then Amy surprised everyone by putting her arm around Bonnie's heaving shoulders, and saying loyally, 'Well, I am not joining in your silly punishment, and I don't care if you send me to Coventry as well! Come along, Bonnie, let's go somewhere where we can be alone.'

With that, she led the weeping girl from the room and, as the door closed behind them, Susan grimaced and said, 'Well, that was simply beastly, but it had to be done.'

Most of the others agreed at once, but Felicity remained silent. She remembered how Bonnie had played a big part in reuniting Julie with her missing horse, Jack, last term. The girl had certainly proved her loyalty to the form then. And there were several other past incidents when Bonnie had shown that, although she could be rather unscrupulous when it came to getting what she wanted, she was absolutely straight and honest – in her own, rather strange way!

Oh dear, thought Felicity, I do hope that we haven't made a dreadful mistake!

A shock for the fourth form

Several days later Felicity and Susan learned some startling news. It was a pleasant, if cold, afternoon, and the two of them were wrapped up in coats, hats and scarves as they walked through the grounds.

'I shall be glad when Bonnie's period of Coventry is over,' said Susan with a sigh. 'It really is horrible. And it is making things awfully difficult as far as the play is concerned, for I can't discuss the costumes with her until I can speak to her again.'

'Yes, but even when we are allowed to speak to Bonnie again, things will never be the same,' said Felicity thoughtfully. 'For this incident will always be at the back of our minds. It's a shame, because although I didn't like Bonnie much when she first came to Malory Towers, I've grown quite fond of her now.'

'Yes, she has many good qualities, although she has a funny way of going about things sometimes,' said Susan. 'Still, I suppose that no one is completely good, or completely bad. And once Bonnie's punishment is over, we shall all have to do our best to try to forget what she has done, and help her try to make amends.'

Just then, the two girls saw a figure coming towards

them, and both groaned inwardly. For it was none other than Miss Tallant!

'Susan!' said the mistress sharply, as she drew level with the two girls. 'I understand that you took a book about play production from my desk yesterday, without permission. Not a very good example for a head-girl to set her form.'

Susan flushed bright red. She had sneaked the book from Miss Tallant's desk, for she knew very well that the mistress did not like her, and would certainly have refused to lend it to her if she had asked.

She had flicked through it in the common-room yesterday evening, and had meant to put it back on Miss Tallant's desk this morning, before the mistress even realised it had gone. But, alas for Susan, she had completely forgotten about it, and now she could have kicked herself!

'Kindly ask permission before borrowing anything again, Susan,' said Miss Tallant coldly. 'And please bring the book to me in the mistresses' common-room before prep this evening.'

'When I will no doubt be given lines, or some other beastly punishment!' muttered Susan as the mistress walked briskly away. 'Blow! Why didn't I remember to put it back this morning?'

'Susan,' said Felicity, with a frown. 'How did Miss Tallant know that you had taken her book?'

'Well, she noticed it wasn't there, I suppose,' said Susan, shrugging.

'Yes, I know *that*,' said Felicity, a little impatiently. 'But how did she know that *you* took it, when it could have been any one of us fourth formers?'

'Golly, I didn't think of that!' exclaimed Susan. 'Well, there is only one explanation. Bonnie must have been tittle-tattling again. Which means that, even after being sent to Coventry, she *still* hasn't learned her lesson! Honestly, that girl is a glutton for punishment!'

'Half a minute, though!' said Felicity. 'Bonnie couldn't have known that it was you who took the book, for she wasn't there when you took it. I was, and so were Pam and Nora – but not Bonnie.'

Susan thought this over for a moment, then said, 'But she *was* in the common-room last night, while I was sitting there reading it. I noticed that she kept glaring across at me, and thought it was because she was still sore at being ignored by everyone. But, of course, she must have been planning to tell on me to Miss Tallant all along.'

Felicity brooded on this as the two girls walked on. They had almost walked as far as the stables, and could see a slim, red-haired girl patting the nose of one of the horses, who had stuck his head over the stable door.

'I say, there's old Clarissa!' cried Susan. 'Hi, Clarissa!'

The girl turned her head, smiling when she saw Felicity and Susan coming towards her. 'Hallo, you two!' she said brightly. 'You only just caught me. I've just been to see Miss Peters, and was about to go back to Five Oaks.'

'How are things at Five Oaks?' asked Susan. 'Bill all right?'

The three chatted together for a while, then Clarissa

said, 'I met that new teacher of yours in town, the other day – Miss Tallant. We had quite a chat.'

'Really?' said Felicity. 'How did you come to meet her, Clarissa?'

'Well, I was in the little tea-shop, waiting for Bill, and Miss Tallant sat down at the table next to mine. I didn't realise who she was at first, of course, but then we fell into conversation. Very pleasant woman!'

Felicity and Susan exchanged startled glances and, noticing this, Clarissa laughed. 'Do I detect that Miss Tallant is not very popular?'

'She's extremely *un*popular!' said Susan, pulling a face.

She and Felicity went on to tell Clarissa about some of the things Miss Tallant had done, and Clarissa exclaimed in surprise. 'Well, I never! She seemed awfully nice when she was talking to me. And, having a niece of her own here, you would think that she would know the best way to handle young girls.'

'A *niece*!' exclaimed the two girls in unison, completely taken aback.

'Well, that's the first we've heard of it!' said Felicity. 'Who is this niece, Clarissa? Which form is she in?'

'Why, the fourth form,' answered Clarissa. 'Apparently she has just started this term.' Clarissa soon went on her way, leaving Felicity and Susan to stare at one another in horror.

'You know what this means, don't you, Felicity?' said Susan in a very serious tone.

'Yes,' said Felicity, also sounding very grave. 'Either

Sylvia or Olive is Miss Tallant's niece. And whichever one of them it is must also be the person who has been sneaking to her.'

'Which means that we accused poor little Bonnie unjustly,' said Susan, with a groan. 'I feel simply dreadful! Felicity, we must round up the others at once, and call a form meeting.'

'Of course,' said Felicity. 'Wait a minute, though! There are two of the others that we don't want at our meeting – Sylvia and Olive themselves. Whichever one of them is the mysterious niece, she obviously doesn't want anyone to know about the connection. And if we ask straight out she is likely to deny it.'

'Yes,' said Susan, looking thoughtful. 'We need to set a trap for her, just as we did for Bonnie. And this time we need to make sure that nothing goes wrong.'

Susan called a meeting of the North Tower fourth formers in one of the music-rooms that evening. Sylvia and Olive, alone in the common-room, wondered where everyone had disappeared to.

'Perhaps there's a debate in the hall, or a slide show, or something,' said Sylvia, sounding puzzled. 'Though I'm quite sure I would have remembered. Do you know where they can all be, Olive?'

Olive shook her head and hoped that Sylvia wasn't going to chatter all evening. She wanted to be alone with her thoughts.

'They can't be holding a rehearsal for the play,' Sylvia went on. 'Or we would have been invited too. Perhaps they're planning some sort of trick, and don't want to let us in on it.'

Olive's ears pricked up at this. 'Perhaps they are,' she said, sounding more friendly. 'Jolly mean of them to leave us out.'

'Well, they know that I'm not awfully fond of jokes and tricks,' said Sylvia. 'I wish that I was, but I never seem to see the funny side of things.'

'I say! Perhaps they are planning to play a trick on us,' said Olive. 'That would explain why they don't want us involved.'

Sylvia looked extremely dismayed at this, and said, 'Surely they wouldn't be so mean?'

'They probably just see it as a bit of fun, and don't think that it's mean at all,' said Olive. 'All the same, after that business with the mouse, I don't really want to be the victim of another of June's pranks. I vote that we go and look for them, Sylvia, and see if we can overhear what they are up to.'

'That seems rather sneaky, don't you think?' said Sylvia, looking rather uncomfortable.

'Nonsense! They are the ones who are being sneaky, plotting things behind our backs,' said Olive. 'Come on, Sylvia! Imagine how uncomfortable you are going to feel tomorrow, knowing that something may be going to happen to you, but not knowing where or when. Why, you'll be on tenterhooks.'

This was quite true. Sylvia really did find the thought of a trick being played on her quite horrid. So, reluctantly, she stood up and said, 'Very well. Let's see if we can track them down.'

But the fourth formers had hidden themselves well. Susan had chosen a music-room right at the top of North Tower, which hardly anybody used. There was no glass in the door, and once all the girls had filed in, she locked the door behind them.

Bonnie had been most surprised to be invited to this meeting, and had said to Susan, 'I thought you weren't supposed to speak to me.'

'Yes, well, I'm afraid there's been a bit of a mis-understanding, Bonnie,' Susan had said, turning red. 'Amy is invited too, of course. I'll explain it all to you both later, at the meeting.'

Bonnie had shrugged, and said, 'You may not get the chance. I don't know if I shall bother turning up.'

And with that, she had walked off, her little nose in the air.

But curiosity had got the better of Bonnie, and now she was in the little music-room with all the others, waiting to hear what Susan had to say.

'It's awfully cramped in here,' complained Amy. 'And it smells dreadfully musty.'

'Well, I shall be as quick as possible,' said Susan. 'Then we can all go back to the comfort of the common-room.'

'I say, Susan, Sylvia and Olive aren't here,' said Julie.

'They weren't invited,' said Felicity. 'And you will understand why, in a moment.'

Swiftly, Susan told the fourth formers what she and

Felicity had learned from Clarissa, and, of course, there was a perfect outcry.

'I wish I knew which one of them it was!'

'Yes, wouldn't I like to tell her what I think of her.'

'To think that she let us blame poor Bonnie,' said June, who was feeling rather ashamed of herself, for she had been the first to accuse Bonnie. She went up to the girl now and held out her hand, saying forthrightly, 'I'm most terribly sorry, Bonnie. I should have known that you wouldn't betray the form like that. I just hope that you will accept my apology.'

Bonnie stared solemnly at June and, for a moment, the others thought that she was going to reject the girl's frank apology. But then she smiled and took June's hand, and a sigh of relief went round the room.

'We are all very sorry, Bonnie,' said Susan. 'We misjudged you badly, and we will all do what we can to make it up to you. Amy, too, for we sent her to Coventry as well. She was the only one who had the good sense to realise that you couldn't possibly have been the sneak, and she was courageous and loyal in sticking by you.'

Amy, unaccustomed to being praised for these good qualities, found herself turning quite pink with pleasure, and graciously inclined her head.

'Well, thank goodness that is sorted out, at least,' said Felicity, thankfully. 'Jolly decent of you to forgive us, Bonnie.'

Bonnie smiled and said, 'I shall expect you all to make it up to me, though, just as Susan said. You are all to be especially nice to me this term.'

'We shall be,' said Pam, giving the girl a pat.

'Bonnie,' said Freddie. 'What *was* the job that you were doing for Miss Tallant? The one that she gave you the chocolate for?'

'It was nothing, really,' said Bonnie. 'She had torn her skirt, and I mended it for her, because she doesn't like sewing. That's all.'

'But why on earth didn't you tell us this in the first place?' said Julie, astonished. 'It would have saved so much unpleasantness.'

Bonnie's little rosebud mouth set in a stubborn line, and she lifted her chin.

'I was cross,' she said. 'Because you thought I was a sneak. And when I get cross I can be awfully stubborn. I thought that you should have believed me, without me having to prove myself.'

'Well, you were quite right,' said Nora. 'But now, the question is, what are we going to do about finding out which of the new girls is Miss Tallant's niece?'

'We shall all have to put our thinking caps on,' said Lucy. 'June, you are usually good at coming up with ideas.'

June, who had been looking rather thoughtful, said, 'I'm afraid someone else will have to think of something, for I have another thing on my mind.'

'What?' asked the others, curiously.

'I'm going to get my own back on Miss Tallant,' said June. 'I don't know how yet, but I'm going to play the biggest, best trick that I have ever played – on her. If only

I knew what her weaknesses are.'

'Well, we know that she doesn't care for mice and spiders, and things like that,' said Felicity.

'Yes, but we have already used those this term,' said June. 'And I do like to be original.'

'There is something that she is even more afraid of,' piped up Bonnie. 'She was talking to me one day when I helped her to tidy the classroom, and I happen to know that Miss Tallant is simply terrified of ghosts.'

'Really?' said June, her quick brain turning over all sorts of ideas instantly. 'How very interesting!'

'How silly of her,' said Susan, rather scornfully. 'There are no such things as ghosts.'

'Well,' said Bonnie. 'Miss Tallant says that she once saw one. It nearly frightened the life out of her.'

'I believe in ghosts,' said Nora, her eyes big and scared-looking. 'I remember once, when I was little –'

'Tell us another time, Nora,' said Susan, who didn't particularly want to spend the rest of the evening in this cramped, musty little room, listening to ghost stories. 'We really should get back to the common-room now, for it won't be long until bedtime.'

She unlocked the door, and the girls filed out. When they reached the bottom of the stairs, Felicity said, 'Now, we must all behave perfectly normally towards Sylvia and Olive for the time being. We don't know which of them is guilty, and it would be terrible if we accused someone wrongly a second time.'

June appeared to have drifted off into a kind of dream,

and Susan said sharply, 'June! Are you listening? We don't want any accusations flying around until we are absolutely certain which of the new girls is the sneak.'

'Of course,' said June. 'Don't worry, Susan, I've learned my lesson. In fact, I wasn't even thinking about the sneak.'

'What *were* you thinking about, June?' asked Freddie, noticing the mischievous glint in her friend's eye.

June grinned, and said, 'I was thinking about the ghost of Malory Towers.'

Miss Tallant strikes again

Sylvia and Olive had returned to the common-room, having failed in their search for the fourth formers. Olive, in particular, felt very disgruntled. She looked across at Sylvia, and thought what a dreadful chatterbox the girl was. Sylvia had kept up a constant stream of talk throughout the search, endlessly speculating on where the girls could be, what they could be doing, and what form any trick they were planning might take. Olive had soon grown heartily tired of her, and thought what bad luck it was that they were thrown together so much.

Just then the door opened, and the rest of the fourth form poured noisily in.

Sylvia and Olive eyed them suspiciously, but Susan grinned warmly and said, 'Did you think that we had got lost?'

'Well, Olive and I did wonder where you had got to,' said Sylvia. 'It's been awfully quiet in here.'

The girls had already decided what story they were going to tell, and Julie said, 'We all popped down to the stables. You see, Lucy has taught her horse Sandy the most marvellous trick. He can count up to five by pawing the ground with his hoof.'

'Yes, I taught him how to do it in the holidays,' said Lucy. 'And, of course, the others were simply dying to see it.'

'I should have liked to see it too,' said Sylvia, looking a little put out. 'I'm very fond of horses, you know.'

'I didn't realise,' said Lucy. 'If I had known I should have asked you to come along too, Sylvia. Never mind, perhaps I can take you to see Sandy tomorrow.'

That cheered Sylvia up, and she was able to dismiss her worries about the girls playing a trick on her. Julie sat down beside her and asked, 'Do you have a horse at home, Sylvia?'

'No, for we don't have any stables,' Sylvia answered. 'My young brother and sister and I go to a local riding school in the holidays, though.'

'How old are your brother and sister?' asked Julie with interest.

Of course, Sylvia needed very little encouragement to talk about herself, and was soon telling Julie all about her home and family.

Felicity, nearby, turned to Susan and said, 'Clever Julie! She is getting Sylvia to talk about her family in the hope that she might let something slip.'

'Good idea!' said Susan. 'If only we could do the same with Olive, but she will just clam up, as she always does.'

'Perhaps the reason she never talks about her family much is because she has something to hide,' suggested Felicity. 'Like an aunt, who also happens to be the most unpopular mistress at Malory Towers.'

'I wouldn't be at all surprised,' said Susan. 'I must

admit, I feel far more inclined to suspect Olive than Sylvia. Sylvia is so open, and will chatter away about herself to anyone who will listen. Hardly the behaviour of someone who is hiding a dark secret!'

'Miss Tallant never seems to take much notice of Sylvia,' observed Felicity thoughtfully. 'Yet she came down hard on Olive over the mouse trick.'

'Did she, though?' said Susan, frowning. 'She may have just pretended to give her a punishment to throw us off the scent. Bonnie said that when she passed the classroom that morning, Olive and Miss Tallant were just talking. Do you remember?'

'Yes,' said Felicity slowly. 'And I've just remembered something else! That photo that Olive put on her locker. I asked her about it, and she bit my head off. She threw it in her locker, in a fit of temper, and I haven't seen it since.'

'What are you getting at, Felicity?' asked Susan, puzzled.

'Well, it looked as if someone was missing from the photograph,' Felicity said. 'Olive's father had his arm outstretched, as though it were around someone's shoulders, but there was no one there. It was as if someone had been cut off. What if that's it, Susan? What if the person missing from the photograph is Miss Tallant?'

Susan gave a gasp, and said, 'I wonder if you could be right, Felicity.'

'Hallo, you two look very serious!' said Pam, coming over with Nora. 'What's up?'

Felicity told the two girls, and Nora said, 'So, it's

looking more and more likely that Olive is the culprit. I must say, I don't altogether blame her for not wanting to own up to having Miss Tallant as an aunt. I certainly wouldn't, if she was mine.'

'Well, we still can't be absolutely certain that it is Olive who is Miss Tallant's niece,' Susan said. 'And until we *are* certain it might be wise to keep our suspicions to ourselves.'

'Yes, I suppose it would,' agreed Pam. 'Actually, Susan, Nora and I came over to ask when we are going to have our first rehearsal. I know it's only short play, and no one has many lines to learn, but we all want it to be perfect.'

'I was thinking about that myself, actually,' said Susan. 'Mary has finished her song, and very good it is too. So now we are just waiting for June and Freddie to add their jokes.' She raised her voice, and called out, 'Hi, June! Freddie!'

The two girls, who were sitting side by side on a sofa, their heads close together as they talked, looked up, and Susan said, 'How are the jokes coming along for our play?'

'Almost finished,' said June, who had thoroughly enjoyed the task that Susan had given her. Ably assisted by Freddie, she had come up with several very funny lines and jokes to add to the script. Now she said, 'Another day or two, and we should be finished.'

'Excellent!' said Susan, happily. 'In that case, we could hold our first rehearsal on Saturday, if the hall is free.'

There were 'oohs' and 'aahs' at this, and Nora clapped her hands together, crying, 'Marvellous! I simply can't wait to begin. Bonnie, how are the costumes coming along?'

'I have made a start on yours, Nora,' answered Bonnie. 'I found the most beautiful dress in the store-room – all white and sparkly. With a little alteration, it will be perfect.'

'I say, I wonder if that was the dress Mary-Lou wore, when she played Cinderella in the pantomime that Darrell wrote,' said Felicity, her eyes shining.

'I'll bet it was,' said Pam. 'My word, that was a jolly good pantomime. I hope our little play will be as big a success.'

'I'm quite determined that it shall be,' said Susan, and everyone agreed.

'We shall spend every spare moment tomorrow finishing our work on the script,' said June to Freddie. 'For once that is done, there is something else I need to concentrate on.'

'How to get back at Miss Tallant?' said Freddie.

'Yes,' said June, her wicked dark eyes glittering. 'My goodness, I'm going to make her wish that she had never crossed me!'

Freddie grinned, and said, 'So, when is the ghost of Malory Towers going to make an appearance?'

'Not until he – or she – is ready,' said June, grinning back at her friend. 'This trick is going to be more carefully planned than any trick I have ever played. I really do intend to give that horrid woman the shock of her life!'

'Well, your brother is coming to see you at half-term, isn't he?' said Freddie. 'He's always full of good ideas, so perhaps the two of you should put your heads together.'

'The *three* of us,' said June. 'Don't forget that you are coming with us at half-term, because your people will be on holiday. And I may need your help, Freddie.'

'You know that you can rely on me,' said Freddie loyally. 'I would like to see Miss Tallant brought down a peg or two as well.'

And Miss Tallant struck again, the day before the first rehearsal was due to take place. The mistress caught Julie whispering to Lucy, and promptly dished out a hundred lines. 'I have to hand them in tomorrow morning!' groaned Lucy. 'And I was hoping to learn my lines for the play tonight.'

'Look here,' said Julie. 'Why don't I do half of them for you, Lucy? My writing is a bit like yours and I bet Miss Tallant will never notice the difference.'

'Oh, would you, Julie?' said Lucy happily. 'You are a sport! If we do them as quickly as we can, we shall both have time to go through our lines.'

The plan was duly carried out, and once the lines were finished, the two girls sat down together in the common-room and read through their parts in the play.

But they were in for a shock the following morning, when Lucy handed two sheets of paper to Miss Tallant, both covered in large, rather sprawling handwriting. The mistress did not even glance at them, but smiled at Lucy, saying, 'I hope that you did not have to waste too much of your evening on these lines, Lucy.'

'No, Miss Tallant,' said Lucy a little nervously.

'Of course you didn't,' said Miss Tallant, her smile

growing broader. 'Because Julie did half of them for you, didn't she?'

Lucy gasped. How on earth could Miss Tallant possibly know *that*? The girls' writing was almost identical, and even if there *was* the very slightest difference, the mistress couldn't have noticed it, for she hadn't so much as glanced at the pages. There was only one way Miss Tallant could know, Lucy realised suddenly, her lips tightening grimly. The sneak had struck again!

Just then, a small second former walked past the classroom, and Miss Tallant called out, 'Elizabeth! Please go and find Julie of the fourth form, and tell her to come to me at once.'

The nervous second former sped off at once, and then Lucy endured a very uncomfortable five minutes indeed! Miss Tallant sat down at her desk and picked up a book, neither looking at Lucy, nor speaking to her. So the girl had to stand in silence, until a puzzled and rather worried-looking Julie arrived. Miss Tallant laid her book aside and got to her feet, and one look at the mistress's face was enough to tell Julie that she was in serious trouble.

'Well, Julie!' said Miss Tallant, looking sternly at the girl. 'I understand that you were foolish enough to help Lucy with her punishment yesterday evening.'

Startled, Julie looked at Lucy. Surely her friend couldn't have been so foolish as to tell Miss Tallant the truth? But Lucy, guessing what Julie was thinking, gave the tiniest shake of her head.

Miss Tallant spoke again, a smile of satisfaction on her face, as she said smoothly, 'Of course, you must both be punished for such deceit. And your punishment will be that you are both forbidden to take part in the rehearsal this afternoon. Instead you will sit here, under my eye, and write an essay on the importance of obeying one's elders and betters.' The girls stared at Miss Tallant in dismay. Julie actually groaned out loud, and opened her mouth to say something, but Lucy gave her a nudge. There was no point in antagonising the mistress, for they would only end up with an even worse punishment. If there *was* anything worse than missing their first rehearsal! They had been looking forward to it so much, and now they were going to miss it. Not only that, but they had let the rest of their form down too, and all through their own deceit.

'I know that what we did was wrong,' said Julie angrily, as the two girls escaped from Miss Tallant's presence, her instructions to come back to the classroom at two o'clock sharp ringing in their ears. 'But we did it for the good of the play, so that you could learn your lines. The mean beast who split on us to Miss Tallant had no good intentions at all!'

'No,' said Lucy miserably. 'She just intended to cause trouble for us with Miss Tallant – *and* to spoil our rehearsal.'

'Well, she has succeeded,' said Julie, who felt very angry and upset.

Felicity and Susan were angry, too, when the two girls

told them that they had been forbidden to attend the rehearsal.

'What rotten luck!' cried Felicity. 'We can't possibly rehearse properly without the whole cast there.'

'Oh, Julie!' wailed Susan. 'I know that you were trying to help, and did it for the good of the play, but I do wish that you hadn't offered to do half of Lucy's lines for her. There are so few characters in the play, that I really don't know if it is worth carrying on with the rehearsal now.'

Julie hung her head and said, 'I'm sorry, Susan. I wish that I hadn't done it now.'

'It's not all our fault, Susan,' said Lucy. 'The person who sneaked on us is to blame, too.'

'I realise that,' said Susan, looking angry. 'But as we don't know who is to blame, we can't deal with them as they deserve.'

'Were both Sylvia and Olive in the common-room last night?' said Felicity, thinking hard.

'Yes, they were,' said Lucy. 'I remember seeing them.'

'Lucy and I were sitting at the table doing our lines,' said Julie. 'I suppose it would have been easy enough for one of them to peep over my shoulder and see that I was helping Lucy. Bother, why couldn't I have been more careful? Susan, you aren't really going to cancel the rehearsal, are you? Do say that you aren't, or I shall feel even more dreadful than I do already.'

'Well, I suppose we shall have to go ahead with it, as all the others are looking forward to it,' said Susan, still sounding rather disgruntled. 'We shall just have to get someone to stand in for you two, though they won't know the lines, of course. For heaven's sake, do take care not to get on the wrong side of Miss Tallant again, for I shouldn't be at all surprised if she is deliberately setting out to spoil our play, simply because we wouldn't let her be involved.'

Fortunately the rehearsal went smoothly, though Olive was not at all happy when Felicity told her that she was going to stand in for Julie, and take the part of the toy soldier.

'Can't you get someone else to do it?' said Olive, sullenly.

'Everyone else is busy with their own parts, or with jobs behind the scenes, so I'm afraid you really have no choice, Olive,' said Felicity firmly. 'And it doesn't matter if you can't act well, because you're only standing in for Julie. All you have to do is read the lines.'

And with that, Felicity pushed a script into Olive's hands and walked away to check that all was well behind the scenes.

A girl called April, from South Tower, was taking Lucy's part – much more graciously than Olive was taking Julie's – and once the two girls joined the rest of the cast on stage, the rehearsal began.

The three producers sat at the front of the hall, and all of them were very pleased with the way things turned out.

There were a few mistakes, of course. Several of the girls fluffed their lines, and Olive somehow managed to trip Nora up during her dance. She hotly denied doing it on purpose, when Nora accused her of this, but most of the girls were quite certain that it had been deliberate.

Susan gave the girl a scold, and Sylvia intervened, saying in a low voice, 'Susan, there's no point in losing your temper. We can't prove that Olive tripped Nora on purpose, and all we're doing is wasting valuable time.' Then she clapped her hands together briskly, and said in her loud voice, 'Come along, girls, back to your places, please, and let's start the dance again. Olive, you stand further back, then if Nora *should* happen to trip again, you can't be held responsible.'

Both Susan and Felicity looked rather taken aback, and none too pleased at this, but as one of the producers, Sylvia was quite within her rights. And both girls had to admit that what she said was very wise and sensible.

The rest of the rehearsal went without mishap, and at the end of it Susan said, 'Well, that wasn't bad at all!'

'I thought that it went very well indeed,' said Sylvia. 'Of course, the girls aren't word perfect yet, but that is only to be expected.'

Felicity, who felt cheered by how well the rehearsal had gone, said, 'You were very good, too, Sylvia. You handled the incident with Nora and Olive perfectly.'

Sylvia shrugged, and said, 'Well, of course, I'm quite an old hand at all of this, you know. Being a former head-girl, and having produced a play myself, I'm used to being a bit of a bossy-boots!'

But both girls noticed that Sylvia had turned pink with pleasure at Felicity's remark and, as she walked away, Susan said, 'Actually, although she can be dreadfully pushy and bossy at times, I think Sylvia is rather nice.'

'So do I,' agreed Felicity. 'And I know it's a horrid thing to say, but I actually *want* Olive to be Miss Tallant's niece, for that would be so much easier to bear than finding out that it is Sylvia.'

'Yes, I feel the same,' said Susan with a sigh. 'What a beastly business it is!'

'Cheer up!' said Felicity, slipping her arm through her friend's. 'There is still an awful lot to look forward to this term, you know. As well as our play, it will be half-term very shortly.'

'So it will!' said Susan, brightening. 'I had almost forgotten about that.'

She chuckled suddenly, and went on, 'And I must say, I'm rather looking forward to finding out how June intends to pay Miss Tallant back. Whatever she has in mind, I'll bet it's something quite ingenious. And I, for one, can't wait to see Miss Tallant get her comeuppance!'

An interesting half-term

The fourth formers took great care not to give Miss Tallant any cause to punish them over the next couple of weeks. They didn't want anyone else missing rehearsals, so they were polite, well-behaved and worked hard in her classes. But, as Pam remarked in the common-room on the evening before half-term, 'She doesn't seem terribly pleased! Any other mistress in the school would be delighted to teach such model schoolgirls.'

'Of course she's not pleased!' said June. 'She *likes* punishing us, and she's disappointed that we haven't given her any opportunity to vent her spite.'

'Well, Miss Tallant might not be pleased, but I certainly am,' said Susan, beaming round. 'Our play is really taking shape, and the last two rehearsals have gone swimmingly.'

'Shh!' hissed Freddie suddenly. 'Sylvia is coming this way, so don't mention Miss Tallant. Change the subject, quickly!'

At once the girls began to talk about the forthcoming half-term, and Sylvia joined in, saying in her hearty way, 'I simply can't tell you how much I am looking forward to my first half-term at Malory Towers, and to showing my people round properly.'

'It's going to be super,' said Julie happily. 'Lucy's parents aren't able to come, so she is coming on a picnic with my people.'

'And I bet Jack and Sandy will be going along too,' laughed Felicity, knowing that the two girls never went anywhere without their beloved horses unless they absolutely had to. Susan glanced round at that moment, and caught sight of Olive, sitting alone, as usual, a sour expression on her plain face.

'Are your people coming tomorrow, Olive?' Susan asked.

'Yes,' answered Olive, in her curiously flat voice. But she volunteered no more information, and discouraged the others from asking any more questions by immediately burying her head in a book. And she didn't look as if she was terribly excited about seeing her family again, thought Susan. She turned to Felicity, and murmured in a low voice, 'I'm jolly well going to keep an eye on Olive and her people tomorrow. If she *is* Miss Tallant's niece, then one of them may give something away.'

'Good idea,' said Felicity. 'And I suppose we had better watch Sylvia's parents too, for we can't rule her out yet.'

But as it turned out, there was no need to watch Sylvia's parents.

The girls leaped out of bed eagerly on the morning of half-term, even lazy Nora, who hated leaving her warm bed on cold mornings.

'Thank heavens it isn't raining,' said June, pulling the curtains open. 'Otherwise the upper-school lacrosse match would have to be cancelled.'

Ruth Grainger, the games captain, had chosen two teams from the upper school to play an exhibition match for the parents, and June had the honour of being the only fourth former to be chosen.

'Just make sure you play up, June!' called out Felicity.

'Yes, we'll all give you three cheers if you shoot a goal,' said Pam.

'I shall do my best,' said June, in her usual off-hand manner. But the others knew that June was as pleased as punch to have been chosen, and felt very proud indeed, though she would never admit it.

After breakfast, Sylvia was called to Miss Grayling's study, and when she returned to the common-room afterwards, she looked so woebegone that the others felt quite alarmed.

'What's up, Sylvia, old girl?' asked Felicity kindly.

'My parents aren't able to come today, after all,' said Sylvia miserably. 'My grandmother has been taken ill, so they have had to go and look after her.'

The others were terribly sorry to hear this, for they knew how disappointed Sylvia must feel.

'I say, what rotten luck!'

'Awfully sorry to hear that, Sylvia.'

'I do hope that your grandmother isn't seriously ill?'

'No, I think it's just a bad dose of flu, but she's too ill to do anything for herself,' answered Sylvia with a sigh. 'Of course, I quite see that Mother and Father have to go to her, but I can't help feeling upset that they won't be here.'

The kindly Pam gave Sylvia a pat on the shoulder, and

said, 'Cheer up, Sylvia! I know it's awful to have news like this at the last minute, but why don't you come out with me and my people instead?'

Sylvia's face lit up and she said, 'Thank you, Pam. That's jolly decent of you, if you're sure your parents won't mind.'

Since Pam's parents were as good-natured and easygoing as their daughter, Pam was able to reassure Sylvia on this point, and the girl cheered up considerably.

'There are some cars coming up the drive!' cried an excited Bonnie, who was peering out of the window. 'Amy, your parents are here! And June, yours are right behind.'

With an excited whoop, June ran from the room, Freddie – who was spending the day with June's people – right behind her. Amy followed at a more dignified pace, while Felicity and Susan went to join Bonnie at the window.

'I do hope my mother and father aren't going to be late,' said Bonnie fretfully. 'They promised to be here early.'

Felicity laughed, and ruffled Bonnie's curly hair. 'Don't worry, Bonnie,' she said. 'Your parents always keep their promises, for you know how to wrap them round your little finger.'

Olive, nearby, muttered under her breath, 'Spoilt brat!' Fortunately for her, no one overheard, for at that moment Bonnie's father's car drew up beneath the window, and the girl squealed loudly in excitement, before darting from the room.

'Someone else's people are here too,' said Susan, leaning out of the window. 'I don't think they belong to anyone here, though, for I don't recognise them.'

Felicity followed Susan's gaze, to where a man and woman were getting out of a car.

With them was a very pretty, dainty girl of about thirteen, with curly golden hair and big eyes.

'The two grown-ups look vaguely familiar to me,' said Felicity. 'Though I don't recognise the girl with them. Oh, I know who they are! Olive, it's your father and step-mother. I remember them from your photograph. Is the girl with them your sister? How pretty she is!'

'She's not my sister!' snapped Olive, her pale skin turning a dull red. 'She's not related to me at all!'

'Well!' exclaimed Nora, as the girl stomped out of the room. 'How odd!'

'Olive *is* odd,' said Susan in disgust. 'Her behaviour gets more peculiar by the day.'

'I wonder who that girl is,' said Felicity. 'Why on earth would Olive's father and step-mother bring someone who isn't related to Olive to visit her at half-term? It doesn't make sense.'

'Oh, who wants to worry about silly old Olive on a day like this?' said Nora. 'If she wants to act all odd and bad-tempered, let her! But I intend to enjoy half-term.'

The others felt exactly the same, and, as more and more parents arrived, went off to greet them excitedly.

Felicity, of course, was delighted to see her own pretty, sensible mother and her tall, distinguished-looking father, and flew into their arms as soon as they got out of the car.

'Mother! Daddy! How super to see you both again!' she

cried. 'Do come and say hallo to Susan and her people.'

Felicity's parents and Susan's parents knew and liked one another, and the two girls were thrilled when both families agreed to join up and go for lunch together at a restaurant.

But before that, there was plenty to see and do.

Parents had to be shown around the dormitory, common-room and classroom, then there were displays of art and needlework to admire, and mistresses to talk to.

Felicity spotted Olive and her family talking to Miss Tallant, and noticed that the mistress was laughing and joking.

'Hmm, that looks very suspicious,' said a low voice behind Felicity. She turned to see that June had come up behind her, and was also watching the little group.

'Miss Tallant spoke to *my* parents a little while ago, and she wasn't nearly as friendly, I can tell you,' June went on. 'Just look how relaxed and jolly she is with Olive's people, though. But then, I suppose she would be if she is related to them!'

'It does look suspicious,' said Felicity. 'Look, she is even talking to the girl that Olive's parents brought with them, as if she is very familiar with her.'

'Well, it looks as if we have discovered who Miss Tallant's niece is,' said June in a hard little voice. 'All we have to do now is catch her out.'

There was no time to say any more just then, for Freddie came over with June's parents, and the four of them went off together.

So Felicity went to join her own parents, who were chatting with Mam'zelle Dupont, feeling rather troubled.

But it was half-term, and Felicity found it impossible to stay troubled for long. Especially when her mother gave her a hug, and said, 'You're doing marvellously, dear. I have had glowing reports of you from every mistress I have spoken to.'

'Yes, Miss Potts said that she is delighted to have you in North Tower,' added Mr Rivers. 'She told me that it is girls like you who makes Malory Towers what it is, for you bring a wonderful spirit to the school. And I must say, darling, I agree with her.'

Felicity felt as if she would burst with pride! Fancy Miss Potts, the strict head of North Tower, saying that about her. She simply couldn't wait to tell Susan.

The two families went off to a restaurant for lunch together, and had an absolutely marvellous time.

'I don't want half-term to end,' said Felicity to Susan, as the two girls tucked into ice-creams. 'What a super day it's been!'

'Well, it's not over yet,' said Susan. 'We still have the lacrosse match this afternoon, then a scrumptious tea to look forward to, and all of tomorrow as well. Marvellous!'

Bonnie was also enjoying herself, for her parents spoiled her dreadfully, hanging on her every word as she chattered away to them. She was taken to a restaurant for lunch too, and was surprised – and none too pleased – to find that Olive and her family had chosen the same one.

'Is anything wrong, darling?' asked Mrs Meadows, noticing Bonnie's frown.

'Oh, it's just that I've seen someone I don't like very much, Mummy,' said Bonnie. 'That girl at the table in the corner. She's in my form and she's simply horrid. No one can bear her.'

'Well, we shall sit as far away from her as possible,' said Mrs Meadows, patting Bonnie's arm. 'What a plain girl she is. Her sister is very pretty, though. Actually, she reminds me a little of you, Bonnie.'

Bonnie hadn't noticed the other girl with Olive, and she looked across at her table again now, spotting the golden-haired girl. Heavens, could that really be Olive's sister? There was absolutely no resemblance between them at all.

'I shouldn't be at all surprised if she was jealous of her sister,' Mrs Meadows was saying now. 'Perhaps that is why she is so horrid to everyone, poor girl.'

'Yes,' said Bonnie, looking thoughtful. 'I think that you may be right, Mummy.' Bonnie watched Olive's family from the corner of her eye as she ate her lunch. Olive remained largely silent throughout, though Bonnie noticed that her father and step-mother addressed a great many remarks to her. But they were treated to the same one-word answers that the Malory Towers girls always got from Olive. The younger girl, however, kept up a stream of bright chatter, much to Olive's evident displeasure, for she scowled constantly.

Bonnie was in a pensive mood on the way back to Malory Towers, and her father glanced at her in the driving mirror, asking, 'Is everything all right, my dear? You're awfully quiet.'

'I'm all right, Daddy,' said Bonnie, smiling angelically at Mr Meadows. 'I was just thinking about something, that's all.'

Bonnie had been thinking about what her mother had said. Mrs Meadows was rather a silly woman at times, but she had a streak of shrewdness in her nature. And Bonnie felt that her mother might have hit the nail on the head with Olive. The girl made up her mind that she was going to try to talk to Olive's sister – if the golden-haired girl *was* her sister – before half-term was over.

And her chance came later that very afternoon. The two girls found themselves side by side while they were watching the lacrosse match. Bonnie disliked all games, and had only brought her parents to watch so that she could support June.

For most of the watching girls, however, it was a thrilling game, and very close. And June proved that she was worthy of being selected for the team by scoring the winning goal in the last minute. While the rest of the fourth formers yelled themselves hoarse, Bonnie clapped politely and heaved a sigh of relief that it was over. And she wasn't the only one, for the golden-haired girl looked relieved too, and the two girls exchanged sympathetic smiles.

As everyone began to move away, Bonnie fell into step beside the girl and said softly, 'I do so hate lacrosse, don't you?'

The girl nodded in agreement, and said in a soft, childish voice, 'I don't like *any* games. Nor does Olive, really. I think she only brought us to watch to spite me, for she knew that I would be simply bored to tears.'

There was a petulant note in the girl's voice, and Bonnie asked, 'Is Olive your sister? You don't look very much alike.'

'Oh no, she's my step-sister,' explained the girl. 'My mother married her father. He's an absolute dear, but Olive simply detests me.'

'Really?' said Bonnie, opening her eyes wide. 'I can't think why.'

'She's horribly jealous of me,' confided the girl, lowering her voice a little. 'You see, she and her father were all-in-all to one another, until Mummy and I came along. Olive simply can't bear it when he pays me any attention.'

She gave a high little giggle, and went on, 'I must admit I do play up to him at times, just to annoy Olive, for I dislike her every bit as much as she dislikes me.'

'She's not an easy person to like,' said Bonnie, wrinkling her nose.

'No, but it is *very* easy to make her lose her temper,' said the girl, pleased that Bonnie seemed to dislike Olive too, and deciding that she was a safe person to confide in. 'And such fun. I like to get her into trouble, too.'

'What kind of things do you do?' asked Bonnie, thinking that this was a very interesting conversation.

'Well,' said the girl. 'Olive deliberately smashed my

favourite doll once, because we had had a row. Of course, I was dreadfully upset, and told Mummy, who insisted that Daddy punish her. He was absolutely furious with her for being so spiteful, and she was sent to bed without any supper that night. Once she had shown that she had a bad temper and a spiteful nature, it was easy. Sometimes things get broken, or go missing, and somehow poor Olive always gets the blame. No one ever suspects that it is me.'

'I see,' said Bonnie. She would have liked to continue talking to the girl, but at that moment her mother called out, 'Annabel! Do hurry up, dear, or we shall be late for tea.' And, with a wave of her dainty little hand, Annabel darted off to catch up with her mother, and Bonnie's own parents appeared, her father saying, 'There you are, Bonnie! You must have fallen behind. Mummy and I thought that we had lost you.'

Bonnie smiled her sweet smile and tucked her hand into the crook of her father's arm, but her thoughts were racing. No wonder poor Olive was so ill-tempered! What a mean-spirited girl Annabel was. And it was quite clear now why Olive despised Bonnie herself, and Nora. The two of them were very like Annabel in looks, though not – Bonnie hoped – in character.

Well, thought Bonnie, quite astonished. Perhaps Olive wasn't as bad as she was painted after all!

Exciting plans

It was a very busy time for the fourth formers once half-term was over. There were rehearsals for the play, of course, with those girls who weren't taking part working hard behind the scenes. Bonnie and her assistants worked like beavers to produce the costumes, those who were good at art helped paint the scenery, and others searched the school from top to bottom for props that could be used.

Then there were school lacrosse matches coming up, and many of the girls were practising hard in the hope that they would be chosen to play.

June and Freddie were full of exciting plans too. They had come back from half-term their eyes alight with mischief, and when Pam had said, 'Oho! What are you two up to?' the two had shaken their heads and replied aggravatingly, 'Wouldn't you like to know!' But they did share one of their plans with the others, in the common-room one evening. Sylvia, who had a sore throat and had gone off to see Matron, was not there. Neither was Olive, who had been called away by Miss Williams over the matter of some poorly written work.

'Gather round, everyone!' cried June. 'With Sylvia and Olive out of the way, it seems as good a time as any to tell you that I intend to hold a midnight feast on my birthday next week, and you are all invited.'

There were 'oohs' and 'aahs' as the fourth formers exchanged excited glances.

'A feast, how thrilling!'

'Yes, we haven't had one in simply ages!'

'We will all bring something, of course, June.'

'Thanks,' said June, beaming round at her friends. 'Mother and Father have given me some money to get what I like, but it won't be enough to feed everyone, so if all you others can bring something, that will be a big help.'

'Jolly decent of you to invite us all, June,' called out Nora.

'Well, that's the thing,' said June. 'I'm *not* inviting all of you. Sylvia and Olive must be kept in the dark for now, for I don't want either of them running off to tell tales to Miss Tallant.'

Then she grinned, and added, 'Actually, that's not quite true. I *do* want the sneak to go to Miss Tallant. But I want to make sure that she tells the *right* tale.'

'What are you planning, June?' asked Felicity.

'I can't say just yet,' said June. 'For Freddie and I haven't quite thought it all out yet. But as soon as we have come up with a way to trick Miss Tallant and her beastly niece, I shall let you know. Personally, I am almost certain that Olive is the culprit.'

Several of the girls murmured in agreement, and everyone looked most surprised when Bonnie piped up, 'I feel rather sorry for Olive.'

'Bonnie, dear, are you feeling quite well?' asked Amy, looking at her little friend in surprise.

'Yes, perhaps you ought to pop along and see Matron, too,' said Nora. 'You're delirious.'

'Nothing of the sort!' said Bonnie. 'It's just that I happened to speak to Olive's step-sister, Annabel, at half-term. And what she told me put quite a different complexion on things.'

'Do tell us,' said June.

So Bonnie told the fourth formers what she had learned from Annabel, and very shocked they looked when she had finished.

'What a mean little beast Annabel sounds!' said Susan, in disgust.

'Poor Olive!' said Pam, her ready sympathy stirred. 'It must be quite dreadful to take the blame for everything that goes wrong, and to know that you are innocent.'

'I daresay it must have seemed to Olive that there was no point in being good and well-behaved,' said Susan, shrewdly. 'So she decided that if she was going to be treated as a bad girl, then she might as well become one.'

Suddenly Felicity snapped her fingers, and cried, 'Of course! The person who is missing from Olive's family photograph isn't Miss Tallant at all! It's Annabel!'

'Yes, that makes sense,' said Susan. 'And to be quite honest, I can't say that I blame Olive for wanting to cut her out.'

'You may be right,' said June. 'But all the evidence still points to Olive being Miss Tallant's niece. And, whatever problems she may have at home with her horrid little step-sister, it doesn't excuse her behaviour towards us.'

'I agree with June,' said Nora. 'I do understand Olive's behaviour a little better now, and I know why she has such a down on Bonnie and me. But, even though I feel sorry for her, the fact remains that we can't trust her.'

Felicity, who had been looking thoughtful, said, 'The best possible outcome of all of this would be for Olive herself to own up that she is Miss Tallant's niece. It would make us all think better of her if she told the truth, and then we could let her know that we felt proud of her for doing the right thing.'

'Marvellous idea!' cried Julie. 'And once we had praised her up a bit, Olive would surely start to feel more confident, and she might find the courage to tell her father about the mean tricks Annabel has been playing.'

Most of the fourth formers thought that this was a very good idea indeed, only June looking rather doubtful.

'If you are all agreed, I will go along with it, of course,' said June. 'But *not* until after the feast, for I'm sure that we are all looking forward to that and we can't risk having it spoiled.'

'That *would* be a terrible shame,' said Lucy. 'I really think that we will have to leave Olive out of it, you know, girls.'

'Yes, I suppose that we better had,' said Susan. 'June, you said that you were working on an idea to trick Olive and Miss Tallant, didn't you?'

'Yes,' answered June. 'If it works, it will keep Miss Tallant nicely out of the way while we enjoy our feast, *and* it will teach Olive that sneaking can sometimes backfire on the sneak, so we shall kill two birds with one stone.'

'That sounds super,' said Susan. 'And once the feast is over, we can all set to work to make Olive own up, and try to set her on the right track.'

Just then the common-room door opened, and in walked Olive, wearing her customary sullen expression.

At once all the girls began to chatter about something else, while Olive sat down in a chair, looking miserably at the returned work that Miss Williams had given her.

Kindly Pam went across to her and said, 'Bad luck, Olive. Those sums that Miss Williams gave us this morning were awfully difficult. I found them quite hard, and I'm not too bad at maths. I say, perhaps I could help you with them?'

For a second it seemed as though Olive was going to bite Pam's head off, but, looking into the girl's friendly, open face, she saw real kindness there and it warmed her. So Olive swallowed her pride, and said, 'Thanks, that's awfully kind of you.'

'Good old Pam,' said Felicity, as she saw the girl sit down next to Olive and begin to patiently explain how best to do the rather complicated sums that Miss Williams had set. 'She really is a decent sort.'

'Yes,' said June. 'Just so long as her decency doesn't carry her away. We don't want Olive turning over a new leaf until *after* the feast!'

Naturally, the feast became the main topic of conversation for the fourth formers. There was a big cupboard just outside the dormitory, which the girls used as a hiding place for all their food. It had a key, which June kept in her pocket at all times so that no one could pry and find the hidden goodies.

The girls were allowed to go into town in their free time, as long as they went in pairs, and June was forever going to the cupboard to hide packets of biscuits, tins of sardines, and bottles of lemonade that one girl or another had brought back with her.

Amy, who had a great deal of pocket money, bought a simply enormous box of chocolates as her contribution to the feast, and she handed them to June when she and Bonnie returned from town.

'Gosh, thanks, Amy!' said June. 'These look simply gorgeous! I'll run up and pop them in the cupboard now, before tea.'

June did so, then she locked the cupboard carefully and slipped the key back into her pocket, before turning to go back downstairs. Then what a shock she had! For Sylvia was standing behind her, and it was quite clear that she must have seen the contents of the cupboard.

June could feel herself turning red, but said breezily, 'Hallo there, Sylvia.'

'Hallo, June,' said Sylvia, her eyes alight with curiosity. 'I say, what on earth is going on? Are you using that cupboard to store food?'

June thought quickly and said, 'Yes, but please don't say anything to anyone, Sylvia. The South Tower girls are planning a feast next week, and they wanted somewhere to store the goodies where their matron wouldn't find them. She's a real nosey-parker, you know, always snooping round, and she's far stricter than our Matron.'

Fortunately, Sylvia, who had never met the placid, good-humoured matron of South Tower, accepted this readily, and said, 'Oh, of course. I shan't say a word.'

June breathed a sigh of relief and went off to tea, catching up with Freddie just as she was entering the dining-room.

'I say!' she whispered. 'I've just had a jolly close shave with Sylvia.'

And, quickly, she told Freddie what had happened.

'That was quick thinking, June,' said Freddie admiringly.

'Wasn't it just?' agreed June, with a cheeky grin. 'And it's given me an idea. How would you like a walk around the grounds before tea, Freddie, old girl?'

Freddie, seeing the gleam of mischief in June's eyes, said at once, 'If I agree, will you tell me what you're up to?'

June nodded, and said, 'Quiet now! Here come the others, and I don't want to let them in on what I'm going to do until I have it all worked out properly.'

It was a chilly evening, and, after tea, the two girls put on their hats and coats, June fetched a torch, and off they went, out into the garden.

'Where are we going?' asked Freddie, curiously.

June glanced over her shoulder, to make sure that no one was around, and said, 'We're going right over in the corner, by South Tower. There is a small gap in the wall there, just big enough for someone to slip through, which leads down to the beach.'

'Is there?' said Freddie, surprised. 'I didn't know that!'

'Hardly anyone does,' said June. 'It's almost completely overgrown by the ivy that hangs down the wall, so it's invisible.'

'Go on,' said Freddie, now very curious indeed.

But June said, 'No, I'll wait until we get there before I tell you what I mean to do. It will be easier to explain if you can see exactly what I mean. Thank heavens that it's a cold evening, and nearly everyone is indoors. No one will be able to see what we are up to.'

But someone *was* about! As the two girls approached the wall, they spotted plump little Mam'zelle Dupont a few yards in front of it.

'Blow!' said Freddie. 'Whatever is Mam'zelle doing here? She likes to be all nice and cosy indoors in the cold weather. It's not like her to take an evening stroll.'

Mam'zelle was well wrapped up in a thick, heavy overcoat, a long woollen scarf around her neck and a fur hat pushed firmly over her neat roll of hair. She was looking a little perplexed, but her face cleared when she saw the two girls, and she cried out, 'Ah, *mes filles*! How happy I am to see you both. You may help me in my search.'

'What are you searching for, Mam'zelle?' asked June.

'My brooch,' answered the French mistress, looking rather unhappy. 'I lost it this afternoon, and now I come to look for it.'

'How can you be sure that you lost it *here*, precisely?' asked Freddie.

'I came this way earlier with Mam'zelle Rougier,' explained Mam'zelle Dupont. 'And I distinctly remember her remarking on how unusual my brooch was shortly before we reached this very spot. Then, when we entered the school, she cried, "Why, Mam'zelle Dupont, your brooch – it is gone!" And so it was – quite vanished. I retraced my steps, but there was no sign of it, so I must have dropped it in the undergrowth here.'

'But, Mam'zelle, why didn't you search for it then, when it was still light?' asked June. 'You don't have a hope of finding it in the dark, especially as you don't even have a torch with you.'

'There was no time then, for I had to teach the third formers,' said Mam'zelle, looking agitated. 'And I see that you have a torch, *ma chère* June. You will switch it on and help me find my brooch, yes?'

Well, this wasn't what the two girls had planned at all, but they couldn't very well say no to the French mistress, so June switched on her torch and played the beam over the bushes that grew next to the wall. Suddenly, her sharp eyes spotted the gap in the wall that she had spoken to Freddie about, and a wicked idea came into her head.

'Here, Freddie,' she said. 'You hold the torch for a bit, and I'll hunt around in the bushes and see if I can spot Mam'zelle's brooch.'

Then, unseen by the French mistress, she winked at Freddie, who wondered what on earth she was up to.

Keeping one eye on Freddie and Mam'zelle, June picked up a stick and poked around in the bushes, then cried, 'I think I see something sparkling – over there!'

Freddie and Mam'zelle both peered in the direction that June had indicated and, quick as a flash, June darted through the little gap in the wall, disappearing from their view.

'I see nothing!' complained Mam'zelle. 'Do you, Freddie?'

'No, not a thing, Mam'zelle,' answered Freddie. 'June, where exactly did you say it was?'

Both she and Mam'zelle Dupont looked towards the spot where June had been standing – but she had gone!

'*Tiens!*' cried Mam'zelle, giving a little start. 'What has happened to June?'

Quick-witted Freddie realised at once what had happened, and distracted Mam'zelle by saying, 'I think I see your brooch down there, Mam'zelle.'

And once again, poor, unsuspecting Mam'zelle, who never seemed to realise when she was having her leg pulled, obligingly turned her head, allowing June to emerge from her hiding place.

'Haven't you found your brooch yet, Mam'zelle?' she asked, and the French mistress spun round sharply, crying, 'There you are, June. Where have you been?'

'Why, nowhere, Mam'zelle,' answered the girl, her lips twitching humorously. 'I've been here all the time. Isn't that so, Freddie?'

Freddie nodded, and Mam'zelle fixed June with a stern

stare, before shaking her head and crying, '*Non! Méchante fille!* You are trying to trick your poor Mam'zelle, once again! I saw you, over there by the wall. I looked away for a split second, and you disappeared – poof!'

'Mam'zelle, I really think that the poor light is making your eyes play tricks on you,' said Freddie, so gravely that June wanted to burst out laughing. 'June most certainly did not disappear.'

'Of course I didn't,' said June. 'You know, Mam'zelle, tricks take quite a lot of planning, and I didn't even know that I was going to bump into you, so I couldn't possibly have prepared anything.'

This gave Mam'zelle pause for thought. She knew how carefully June worked out her tricks, and the girls had come upon her quite by chance. So, she was forced to agree that, in the gathering gloom, her eyes had indeed deceived her.

'And still I have not found my brooch,' she said, rather forlornly. 'It is a very special one, for my nephew gave me it for my birthday.'

Freddie, who, like most of the other girls, was very fond of Mam'zelle Dupont, felt sorry for her, and said kindly, 'Look here, Mam'zelle, why don't you go indoors and get warm? June and I will carry on looking for your brooch, and we will come and tell you if we find it.'

'Ah, you are indeed good, kind girls!' cried Mam'zelle, quite forgetting that, a few moments ago, she had accused June of tricking her. The thought of going indoors and sitting before a roaring fire, with a mug of hot cocoa, was so pleasant that she could almost have hugged the two girls.

June was less pleased, though, and said rather crossly to Freddie, 'Why on earth did you volunteer us to find Mam'zelle's brooch? It's getting jolly cold now, and I was looking forward to sitting in the common-room for a bit, now that we've done what we came for.'

'I know, but poor old Mam'zelle looked so miserable,' said Freddie, who was much more soft-hearted than her friend. 'The brooch must be around here somewhere, so if we hurry up and find it we'll still have time for a sit down before prep. Besides, after the trick you played on Mam'zelle, I think that the least we can do is help her.'

June grinned at this, and said, 'Yes, I suppose you're right. Did it really look as if I had vanished into thin air, Freddie?'

Freddie nodded and gave a shiver, 'It was quite creepy, actually, the way you suddenly disappeared and then reappeared again.'

'Good,' said June. 'I was hoping you would say that, for I intend to give Miss Tallant the fright of her life! Let me tell you what I am going to do.'

As the two girls talked, they began to hunt for the missing brooch. In a very short time their efforts were rewarded. Freddie gave a cry and yelled, 'I've found it! My word, won't Mam'zelle be pleased?'

Mam'zelle was highly delighted when June and Freddie took the brooch to her, patting the girls on their shoulders.

'Ah, you may be bad sometimes, but you are good girls

at heart!' she cried, beaming at the two girls. 'I only wish that there was some little reward I could give you.'

'There is, Mam'zelle,' said June promptly. 'You can let the two of us off French prep for a week.'

But even big-hearted Mam'zelle was not that generous, and she wagged her finger at June, saying, 'Now you try to take advantage of me! One minute you are good, June, and the next you are bad again! I do not know whether I am on my heels or my head with you! But I shall not forget the favour that you and the dear Freddie have done me, and you may be sure that I shall think of something I can do to repay you.'

A trap is set

And Mam'zelle was as good as her word, for a few days later, when the girls were at tea, the French mistress produced the most enormous chocolate cake, which she placed in the centre of the fourth form's table.

'Heavens, Mam'zelle, that looks simply delicious!' said Nora. 'What have we done to deserve this?'

'You have June and Freddie to thank,' said Mam'zelle, cutting the cake into big slices. 'They found my brooch the other day, and I promised them a reward.'

'Jolly decent of you, Mam'zelle,' said Freddie.

'Yes, thanks, Mam'zelle,' said June. 'Though I don't see why the others should share it, for they did nothing. Really, Freddie and I should have half each.'

Of course, June was joking, and the others laughed as Mam'zelle handed round slices of cake, Lucy saying, 'Good show, June and Freddie! Mam'zelle, you should lose your jewellery more often, if this is what happens.'

'I say, June!' said Sylvia, who was sitting beside the girl. 'Speaking of cake, that was a fine, big fruit cake that I saw you put in the cupboard this morning. My word, the South Tower girls must have enough food to feed an army.'

'Sh! Keep your voice down, Sylvia!' hissed June. 'Do you want Mam'zelle to overhear, and spoil the feast for the South Tower girls?'

'Sorry, June,' said Sylvia, lowering her voice and looking rather sheepish.

But Felicity and Susan, on the opposite side of the table, had heard Sylvia's remark and were puzzled by it. What on earth did Sylvia mean about the cake that the two of them had bought being meant for the South Tower girls' feast?

They caught up with June after tea and asked her about it.

'Sylvia caught me stowing some food in the cupboard,' explained June. 'I told her that the South Tower girls were having a feast to throw her off the scent. And I'm going to make sure that Olive thinks the same. Then whichever of the two girls is our sneak is sure to tell Miss Tallant.'

'So she will be thrown off the scent, too,' said Susan. 'And we can have our feast in peace, because Miss Tallant will be over at South Tower on a wild goose chase!'

'June, what a super idea!' laughed Felicity. 'I would love to see Miss Tallant burst into South Tower to spoil the feast, only to find the girls tucked up in bed. How foolish she is going to look!'

'That is going to be the least of Miss Tallant's problems,' said June, with a wicked grin. 'Just wait and see what I have in store for her!'

'June, do tell!' begged Felicity and Susan.

'I shall tell you, but not now,' promised June. 'I have

something else to do at the moment. Has anyone seen Bonnie?'

June eventually found Bonnie in the dormitory, where she was brushing out her curly hair in front of a mirror.

'Bonnie,' said June. 'Thank goodness I've found you.'

Bonnie looked round at the girl in surprise, and said in her lisping voice, 'Is something the matter, June?'

'Not exactly,' answered June, sitting on the edge of one of the beds. 'But I need you to do something for me. I want you to help me set up this trick that I'm going to play on Miss Tallant.'

Bonnie clapped her hands together in glee, and said, 'Goody! Just tell me what you want me to do, June.'

'Well, Bonnie,' began June. 'I know that you talk to Miss Tallant a lot, and I want you to tell her a little story – all about the ghost of Malory Towers.'

'Ooh!' said Bonnie, thrilled, her big eyes growing wide. '*Is* there a ghost at Malory Towers, June?'

'Not as far as I know,' said June, grinning at Bonnie. 'But we are going to make Miss Tallant *think* that there is! Next time you have a chance to speak to her in private, Bonnie, I want you to tell her that you woke up in the middle of the night and went to look out of the window. And you saw a pale, ghostly figure over by South Tower.'

Bonnie was so excited that she couldn't speak, but she nodded vigorously, and June went on, 'Tell Miss Tallant that it looked up at you watching from the window, then disappeared into thin air.'

'Yes, I can do that, all right, June,' said Bonnie, eagerly. 'Anything else?'

'Yes,' said June. 'I think it would be a good idea if we were to make up a tragic story about a young girl who died at Malory Towers many, many years ago, and whose spirit is said to haunt the school.'

'We could say that she died by falling off the cliff!' cried Bonnie, struck by sudden inspiration.

'Brilliant!' said June. 'Yes, I see it all. She quarrelled bitterly with her sister, and was so upset that, one dark, stormy night, she ran away. But the wind was so fierce that it blew out the lantern she carried with her and, in the pitch darkness, she stumbled off the cliff.'

'Oh, the poor, poor girl!' cried Bonnie, looking as if she was about to burst into tears.

'Ass!' said June, giving her a shove. 'It's only a story, remember!'

'Yes, but you told it so convincingly, June, that I felt quite moved,' sighed Bonnie. 'And I think I know what comes next. The girl's tormented, restless spirit haunts the school, seeking out her sister so that they can make up their quarrel.'

'Actually I hadn't thought of that, but it's very good,' said June approvingly.

'I shall tell Miss Tallant tomorrow that I saw the ghost,' said Bonnie. 'Just to unsettle her a little. Then, the next day, I shall tell her the story of the dead girl. I really think that she will be frightened, June, because of the ghost that she saw when she was younger.'

June, who was far too down-to-earth to believe in ghosts, gave a snort, and said, 'I daresay it was a shadow, or a trick of the light. But it's a jolly good thing that it happened, for it has given us a way to punish Miss Tallant for being so mean to the fourth form.'

Bonnie carried out her part of the plan faithfully, and had the satisfaction of seeing Miss Tallant's face turn white as she told her tale.

'She looked like a ghost herself,' laughed Bonnie, as she related what had happened to June and Freddie.

'Well done, Bonnie,' said June, pleased with the girl. 'And now, Freddie, we must make preparations to carry out *our* part of the plan.'

There was a rehearsal for the play that afternoon, and Bonnie, in her role of wardrobe mistress, was most surprised when June and Freddie came backstage and began showing a great interest in the costumes, wigs and greasepaint that were there.

'I say, June!' called out Freddie. 'This would be simply perfect.'

Freddie was holding up an old-fashioned, white night-dress, and Bonnie gave a squeal.

'Freddie Holmes, if you get dirty finger-marks on that, I shall never forgive you!' she said. 'That's Molly's costume and I have just had it washed.'

'Bonnie, dear,' said June, putting an arm round the girl's shoulders. 'May I borrow it, please?'

'Whatever for?' asked Bonnie, puzzled. 'You have perfectly good pyjamas of your own.'

'I don't want to wear it to bed,' chuckled June. 'You see, Bonnie, I am going to dress up as a ghost, and scare the living daylights out of Miss Tallant!'

'When?' asked Bonnie.

'On the night of our feast,' said June. 'You see, she is going to be under the impression that the South Tower fourth formers are holding a feast, and she will rush over there at midnight to stop it. But Freddie and I are going to prepare a little surprise for her.'

Bonnie was torn. On the one hand, she felt quite thrilled at the thought of the unpleasant Miss Tallant being punished for her nasty ways. On the other, the thought of the exquisite nightdress that she had painstakingly altered to fit Molly becoming damaged or dirty quite filled her with horror.

As though sensing what she was thinking, June said, 'I promise that I shall take great care of it, Bonnie, and if it should become dirty I will wash it myself.'

'Very well,' said Bonnie, at last, handing the nightdress over. 'And just see that you *do* take care of it, June.'

'We could borrow some of this greasepaint, too,' said Freddie. 'The white one would give you a ghostly pallor, June, and we could use this purple one to make dark hollows under your eyes.'

'Good idea!' said June.

'And you could really do with a wig,' said Bonnie. 'For you don't want to run the risk of Miss Tallant recognising you. Try this.'

And Bonnie picked up a long, dark wig, which she put on June's head.

'Marvellous!' said Freddie, happily. 'With the wig and some greasepaint, I really don't think that your own mother would know you, June.'

When the rehearsal was over, June and Freddie ran up to the dormitory with the things that they had found for June's disguise, and hid everything away carefully.

As they walked out on to the landing, June spotted Olive coming up the stairs, and, putting a finger to her lips, quickly pulled Freddie into an alcove. Then she waited until Olive had gone into the dormitory, leaving the door open behind her. Beckoning to Freddie to follow, June went over to the cupboard where the food for the feast was being stored.

Unlocking the door, and opening it with a lot of quite unnecessary noise, June said loudly, 'My word, what a lot of food! Those South Tower girls are going to have a marvellous feast.'

Following June's lead, Freddie said, 'What a pity that we can't join them, for it all looks super. Thank goodness we were able to help them out by storing their food for them. When did you say that they are holding the feast, June?'

'On Friday night, at midnight exactly,' said June, in her clear voice, as she locked the door again.

The two girls walked away, and as they reached the bottom of the stairs, June said, 'Well, Miss Tallant is bound to get the false information now, either from Olive or Sylvia. Everything is working out perfectly!'

Friday was June's birthday, and most of the girls had bought her a little gift of some sort.

Felicity gave her a bottle of bath salts, and Susan gave her an enormous bar of chocolate.

Freddie, who had noticed that June's old purse was looking very shabby indeed, had bought her a new one, while Bonnie presented her with a set of handkerchiefs that she had embroidered herself. The only person who didn't give June a present was Olive, but as June said, 'I didn't really expect anything from her. And, to be honest, I'm quite glad that she didn't give me anything, for I shouldn't have liked to have accepted a gift from someone I don't like, and who I believe to be a sneak.'

'Well, you've had some jolly nice presents, anyway,' said Nora, looking rather enviously at the things June had received.

'Yes, thanks awfully everyone,' said June, smiling round at her friends. 'You've all been very generous.'

'And the best part of your birthday is still to come,' said Freddie, in a low voice. 'The feast tonight.'

'Yes,' said June, looking round to make sure that Sylvia and Olive could not overhear. 'I don't know which I'm looking forward to most – that, or the trick that we are going to play on Miss Tallant.'

Felicity and Susan, standing nearby, *did* overhear, though, and Felicity said at once, 'Is the ghost of Malory Towers going to make an appearance tonight, then?'

'She certainly is,' said June, her eyes sparkling with mischief. 'She's going to appear in the grounds, while Miss Tallant is making her way to South Tower. And then she is going to vanish again.'

'But June, you'll miss your own birthday feast if you are out in the grounds playing a trick on Miss Tallant,' said Felicity, with a frown.

'No, I shan't,' said June. 'Freddie and I are going to wake up before you others, so that I can get dressed up in my ghost costume. And the actual trick itself will only take a few moments, so we shall be back in the common-room with the rest of you in a trice.'

'What a pity that we shan't all be there to see the trick,' said Susan with a sigh. 'I should love to see Miss Tallant's face when she sees the ghost!'

'Well, Freddie and I will tell you all about it,' promised June.

'What about Sylvia and Olive?' said Felicity, looking worried. 'One of them is Miss Tallant's niece, and the sneak, and if she wakes up and finds us out of our beds she is bound to cause trouble for us.'

'Oh, I've thought about that,' said June coolly. 'Just make sure that whoever is last out of the dormitory locks the door behind them.'

Susan gave a gasp, and said, 'June, we can't do that!'

'We must,' said June firmly. 'Probably neither of them *will* wake up and everything will be all right, but I don't want to take any chances. Of course, if they should happen to wake, tomorrow the sneak will probably tell Miss Tallant about the feast, but by then it will be too late. It will simply be our word against her niece's. And Miss Tallant's niece is not going to be in her good books, for having sent her over to South Tower for nothing.'

'That's true,' said Felicity. 'I must say, I'm still not entirely happy about locking the two of them in the dorm, but it would be too bad if the feast was spoiled.'

As things turned out, there was no question of locking Sylvia in the dormitory, for later that day she was sent to Matron by Miss Williams.

'Sylvia will be spending a couple of days in the San,' Miss Williams informed her class that afternoon. 'The poor girl has had a dreadful sore throat for several days now, and she has quite a temperature.'

'Poor old Sylvia!' said Pam. 'I thought that she didn't look very well earlier on.'

Everyone was sorry to hear that Sylvia was ill, but as Lucy said to Julie, 'At least it means that she is safely out of the way now, and won't have to be locked in the dormitory with Olive.'

Most of the fourth formers now knew of the plan to lock Olive in the dormitory while the feast took place, and they also knew that June meant to give Miss Tallant a scare.

Everyone was very excited, and found it hard to keep their mind on lessons that day.

'Nora!' said Miss Williams sharply, in the maths lesson. 'Is your knowledge of the maths that we are doing so great that you can afford to waste time by whispering to Pam?'

'No, Miss Williams,' said Nora meekly.

'Then kindly pay attention to what I am saying,' said the mistress. 'Unless you want to come to me for extra coaching after tea?'

Nora didn't want that at all, so she bent her head over her book and did her best to concentrate for the rest of the lesson.

Bonnie also found her mind wandering in French, but as she was one of Mam'zelle Dupont's favourites, she found it quite easy to talk her way out of trouble.

'*Ma chère* Bonnie, you are restless!' complained Mam'zelle. 'You do not concentrate. What is the matter with you?'

Bonnie turned her large, brown eyes on the French mistress, and said in a sad tone, 'I'm sorry, Mam'zelle. You know how much I love your French lessons, but I am just so worried about poor Sylvia. I expect you have heard that she has been taken ill.'

Of course, Bonnie had not been thinking about Sylvia at all. She had been thinking about the midnight feast, and the trick that June was going to play on Miss Tallant. But Mam'zelle, as usual, was quite taken in, and cried, 'Ah, it is kind of you to be concerned for *la pauvre* Sylvia. But you must not worry your head, Bonnie, for Matron will take the greatest care of her.'

Olive, hearing this, threw an angry glance in the girl's direction. If it wasn't just like Bonnie to worm her way out of trouble! She was just like her beastly step-sister, Annabel, and how Olive detested them both.

Surprisingly, though, no one was scolded in Miss Tallant's class. Julie and Lucy whispered together, and June flipped a paper dart at Olive, but Miss Tallant, for once, didn't even notice, seeming quite preoccupied.

'She was thinking of tonight, I expect,' said June scornfully, once the lesson was over.

'And of how she is going to ruin things for the South Tower girls.'

'What a shock she is going to get!' laughed Nora. 'My word, I simply can't wait for tonight to come!'

The ghost of Malory Towers

Some of the girls found it very hard to get to sleep that night, for they were all thoroughly overexcited. At last, one by one, they dropped off. Susan, who was to be responsible for waking the girls in time for the feast, had set her alarm clock for ten minutes to midnight. She had placed it under her pillow, so that the sound did not disturb Olive. June also had an alarm clock under her pillow, but hers was set for half past eleven. When it went off, she awoke at once, and nudged Freddie, in the next bed. The two girls got out of bed, then put bolsters down the middle of their beds, just in case Matron or one of the mistresses should peep in.

The things that they needed for June's disguise were in a box under her bed, and she picked it up. Then the two girls tiptoed silently from the room, and went into a little bathroom at the end of the corridor.

There, they worked swiftly. Freddie rubbed the white greasepaint all over June's face, then carefully smudged some of the purple around her eyes.

'Golly!' said Freddie, standing back to admire her handiwork. 'You look simply ghastly!'

'Thank you,' said June with a grin.

Then June changed into the long, white nightdress, pulling it very carefully over her head, so as not to get greasepaint on it.

'Bonnie will be simply wild with me if I get it dirty,' she said.

Finally, she placed the wig on her head, smoothing the hair into place, and Freddie said, 'Thank goodness it's not windy tonight. It really would give the game away if your wig blew off!'

But it was a perfectly calm, still night as the two girls crept out of a side door and, under cover of the trees, made their way to South Tower.

There, they crouched behind a hedge, and Freddie whispered, 'It's five minutes to midnight. Do you suppose that Miss Tallant is already in South Tower?'

'No,' whispered June. 'She thinks that the feast is starting at midnight, and she will want to catch the girls in the act. I think that she will appear shortly after midnight. Freddie, I'm going to take my place now. You know what you need to do.'

'You can count on me, June,' said Freddie solemnly. 'Now, off you go.'

June darted over to the wall, slipping swiftly through the hidden gap there and disappearing from view. Freddie, still in her hiding-place, gave a shiver. June really did look like a very realistic ghost, and watching her vanish like that was very creepy indeed! The night was cold, and Freddie hoped that they would not have to wait too long for Miss Tallant to arrive.

But, as June had predicted, the mistress came into view shortly after midnight, looking over her shoulder with many nervous glances as she approached South Tower. Freddie grinned to herself in the darkness. Miss Tallant was no doubt thinking of Bonnie's ghost story, for she was evidently very uneasy indeed.

Freddie crouched down lower, to make sure that the mistress couldn't possibly spot her, then she let out a high-pitched wail. This was both to scare Miss Tallant, and to warn June that their victim had arrived. And the unearthly wail certainly succeeded in its first objective, for the mistress jumped violently, and put a hand to her heart.

'Who is there?' she demanded, her voice quavering.

But no answer came and, with one last, scared look round, Miss Tallant put her head down and strode briskly into South Tower.

With the mistress safely out of earshot, Freddie gave a low whistle, which told June that Miss Tallant had gone inside. Now, all they had to do was wait.

Five minutes later, a red-faced Miss Tallant emerged, escorted to the door by Miss Markham, the stern head of South Tower.

Miss Markham looked even sterner than usual, and her voice carried on the still night air to the listening Freddie.

'I find your behaviour quite extraordinary, Miss Tallant,' the mistress said coldly. 'If you had reason to suspect that my girls were holding a midnight feast, you should have come to me, instead of bursting into their dormitory like that and waking them all up. I don't feel that Miss Grayling will be impressed by your conduct.'

Miss Tallant mumbled something which might have been an apology, then Miss Markham bade her a frosty goodnight, before going back inside and closing the door.

Freddie put a hand over her mouth to stifle her laughter at the mistress's disgruntled expression. The person who had wrongly informed Miss Tallant that there was to be a feast in South Tower was certainly going to get it tomorrow!

As Miss Tallant moved forward, Freddie let out another wail, which stopped the mistress in her tracks. And this was the signal for June to come out. She slid silently through the gap in the wall, standing several yards from Miss Tallant.

And Miss Tallant, rooted to the spot in terror, was too frightened even to scream as she stared at the apparition before her, with its deathly pallor and big, hollow eyes.

June took a small step in the direction of Miss Tallant, who let out a sound between a moan and a whimper, then she turned away and vanished through the gap again.

Miss Tallant remained frozen in horror for a moment, then she let out a piercing shriek, so loud that both June and Freddie had to clap their hands over their ears.

Miss Markham, who had just reached her bedroom, gave a start and quickly made her way downstairs and outside again, where she found a pale, trembling Miss Tallant.

'Good heavens!' cried Miss Markham. 'What on earth has happened, Miss Tallant?'

'A g-ghost!' stammered Miss Tallant. 'I – I saw a ghost!'

Miss Markham, who had long ago sized Miss Tallant up as a rather silly, spiteful woman, pursed her lips. She knew that there were no such things as ghosts, and would very much have liked to give the mistress a piece of her mind. But there was no doubt that the woman had suffered a great shock, for she was as white as a sheet, and was shaking from head to foot. Miss Markham said crisply, 'I daresay that your imagination was playing tricks on you, Miss Tallant. Still, it is quite clear that you cannot return to North Tower in this state. Come up to my room, and I shall make you some hot cocoa, and then I will walk back to North Tower with you.'

Miss Tallant was only too happy to let Miss Markham lead her inside, and as soon as the two mistresses had disappeared, Freddie crept out from behind the hedge, and went across to the wall.

'June come out!' she hissed. 'Let's get back to North Tower quickly, while Miss Tallant and Miss Markham are both inside.'

The ghostly June emerged, her enormous grin making her look even more frightening than she had before, as she said, 'That went well. Did you see her face, Freddie?'

'Yes, but do hurry, June,' begged Freddie, taking her friend's arm and beginning to run. 'The feast will have started by now, and I don't want to miss another minute of it. I don't know why, but this midnight haunting has made me awfully hungry!'

The feast had indeed started, and the fourth formers were enjoying themselves enormously.

Susan had gone round quickly and quietly, waking everyone up and taking great care not to disturb the sleeping Olive. June had given Susan the key to the store cupboard, and she, Felicity, Pam and Nora had got all the food out, while the rest of the girls put on dressing-gowns and slippers and padded down to the common-room.

Then Susan had taken a last look into the dormitory to make sure that Olive was still asleep, before locking the door behind her and following the others downstairs.

Someone had lit candles and closed the heavy curtains, so that nothing could be seen from outside. Bonnie, who was a great favourite with the kitchen staff, had coaxed the cook into lending her some plates and cups, and the girls set everything out on them.

Then Felicity said, 'It doesn't seem right starting until June gets here. It is her birthday feast, after all.'

'Yes, but she did tell us not to wait,' said Susan, eyeing the plates of food longingly.

How delicious everything looked! There was an enormous pork pie, biscuits, tins of sardines and pineapple, cake, chocolate and all kinds of goodies!

'She won't be very long,' said Julie. 'And we shall make sure that there is plenty left for her, and for Freddie.'

So the girls munched away happily, all the time wondering what was happening to June and Freddie.

'I do hope that the trick went well,' said Lucy. 'My

goodness, wouldn't it be dreadful if they got caught!'

'June won't get caught,' said Bonnie confidently. 'She always plans everything so carefully.'

And it was soon seen that Bonnie was quite right, for June and Freddie joined them, and the girls gasped to see June dressed up as a ghost.

Bonnie and Amy shrieked so loudly that Susan had to tick them off.

'Idiots!' she hissed. 'Do you want to wake up the whole of North Tower?'

'Sorry, Susan,' said Bonnie. 'But really, June looks so frightening that I simply couldn't help myself.'

June grinned and said, 'Miss Tallant screamed too – much more loudly than you, Bonnie.'

She and Freddie sat down and began to eat, while the fourth formers clamoured to know what had happened.

Assisted by Freddie, June told them, and the listening girls gasped as June told the tale.

'Well!' said Pam. 'All the years I've been at Malory Towers, and I didn't know that there was a gap in the wall by South Tower.'

'Well, we fourth formers will keep it to ourselves,' said Susan. 'Who knows when we may need to use it again.'

'I expect Miss Markham will be bringing Miss Tallant back to North Tower soon,' said Freddie, tucking into a slice of pork pie. 'But we have nothing to fear, because her room is at the other side of the building, and she will come in at the door over there.'

'Perhaps I should go and wait for her,' said June, with

a smile. 'Just to see her jump out of her skin.'

The others laughed at this, but Susan said, 'I don't think we had better risk any more wandering around. It's jolly lucky that you two didn't get caught outside, June and Freddie, for you know that there is a strict rule forbidding any girl to leave her tower at night.'

'I wonder if dear Olive is still sleeping peacefully?' said Amy.

'She must be,' said Nora. 'Or we should have heard her banging at the dormitory door by now.'

'Gosh, I never thought of that,' said Felicity, looking alarmed. 'What are we to do if she starts banging at the door?'

'I suppose I shall have to go up and unlock the door,' said Susan with a grimace. 'And then I will have to tell Olive why she wasn't invited to our feast, and warn her what will happen if she splits on us.'

But there was not a sound to be heard from upstairs, and the girls finished their feast in peace, until there was hardly anything left. Then they sat around eating the chocolates, finishing the lemonade and chatting idly.

At last, Susan said, 'I suppose we had better clear up now.'

Nora gave a groan and said, 'This is the part of midnight feasts that I always hate.'

'Come on, lazybones,' said Pam, giving her a nudge. 'If we all pitch in, it shouldn't take long.'

So the fourth formers got to work, sweeping up the crumbs, piling up the plates and collecting up the empty lemonade bottles. Lucy put them into a cupboard, saying, 'I'll get rid of these tomorrow.'

'And I will take the plates and cups back to Cook in the morning,' said Bonnie. 'My goodness, my first midnight feast! What fun it's been!'

Everyone agreed to that, as, tired and happy, they tiptoed upstairs. Susan unlocked the door very quietly, feeling relieved when she saw that Olive was still fast asleep and didn't appear to have stirred. Tomorrow, she thought, getting into bed, she would have to try and think of a way of getting either Olive or Sylvia to own up to being Miss Tallant's niece. But, at the moment, she was just too tired to think, falling asleep almost as soon as her head touched the pillow. So did the others, for it had been a very tiring evening and they were quite worn out.

And all of them had great difficulty in getting up the following morning! Olive, who was awake bright and early, simply couldn't understand why the others were so sluggish.

Even Julie and Lucy, who liked to race down to the stables before breakfast to see their horses, couldn't get out of bed. At last, Susan sat up and said, 'Come on, girls, we must get a move on or we shall be late for breakfast.'

There were moans and groans at this, but most of the girls got out of bed and began to get ready. Only Amy and Nora stayed put, but they always hated getting up anyway.

'I don't want any breakfast,' muttered Amy, turning over and closing her eyes. 'I would much rather have an extra hour in bed.'

'Amy, it doesn't matter whether you actually *want* breakfast or not, you must put in an appearance, or Miss Williams will come looking for you,' said Felicity. 'And if she finds you in bed, it will mean an order mark against the whole form.'

'The same goes for you, Nora,' said Pam to her friend. 'Do get up.'

'I can't!' wailed Nora. 'I feel sick.'

'Well, it jolly well serves you right for eating six chocolate biscuits,' said Pam, bending her head close to Nora's, so that Olive could not overhear. 'Do come along now!'

At last everyone was ready, and the girls trooped down to breakfast. They cast several interested glances Miss Tallant's way, for all of them were curious to know how she was feeling after her ordeal last night.

She looked very pale indeed, and there were dark circles under her eyes, as though she had not slept well.

June noticed too, with satisfaction, that her hand shook slightly as she picked up her cup of tea. She pointed this out to Freddie, who said, 'Serves her right. At least she won't be snooping around at night in future. I shouldn't be at all surprised if she is afraid to leave her bedroom now!'

None of the girls ate very much breakfast, for they all felt full from the feast the night before, and one or two of them really did feel sick. Mam'zelle Dupont, at the head of the table, looked quite concerned when Nora refused to eat her toast, saying, 'Ah, *la pauvre*! You are sick. You shall go to Matron immediately.'

But Nora had no intention of doing this, for Matron had a knack of knowing when a midnight feast had been held, and kept a bottle of especially nasty-tasting medicine for anyone who complained of feeling ill afterwards. So, to put Mam'zelle's mind at rest, the girl nibbled at a corner of her toast and sipped a cup of tea.

It was as the girls were leaving the dining-room that Miss Tallant approached them and snapped, 'Olive! I want a word with you.'

The listening fourth formers noticed how the girl turned pale, and stammered, 'But Miss Tallant, I have to take some work to Miss Williams.'

'Come and see me immediately afterwards,' said the mistress, a cold, angry look on her face. 'And please don't keep me waiting!'

Olive went off to find the work that she had to give to Miss Williams, looking very unhappy, and the others exchanged glances.

'Well!' said June, raising her dark eyebrows. 'I'll bet you anything you like that Miss Tallant is going to give Olive a scold for sending her on a wild goose chase last night.'

'Yes, I think you're right,' said Felicity. 'It looks as if Olive is her niece all right. And I wouldn't like to be in her shoes when she faces her aunt!'

'I've been trying to think of a way to get her to own up,' said Susan. 'But I really can't.'

'Well, let's have a try in the common-room later,' said Pam. 'And if she won't admit to being Miss Tallant's niece and sneaking on us, then we will just have to tackle her about it, I'm afraid.'

As it was Saturday, there were no lessons, but a rehearsal for the play was scheduled for the afternoon. And several of the girls thought that it would be a nice idea to go and see Sylvia.

'Let's pop across to the San now,' said Felicity to Susan. 'I think that there is a bar of chocolate in the common-room, left over from the feast. Perhaps if we take it to her it might cheer her up a bit.'

'Good idea,' said Susan. 'I feel a lot happier about visiting her now that we know for certain that she isn't the sneak.'

So the two girls went into the common-room to fetch the chocolate, then went along to the San. But they were in for a shock!

Miss Tallant's niece

'Hallo, girls,' said Matron to Felicity and Susan, as they entered the San. 'Come to see Sylvia? Well, she is feeling a little better today, and I daresay a visit will cheer her up.' They found the invalid sitting up in bed reading a book, and looking rather down in the dumps. But she brightened when she saw her visitors and put the book aside, saying in a rather croaky voice, 'Do come and sit down! You can't imagine how marvellous it is to see you. Matron is a dear, but –'

'But she can be awfully bossy at times,' Felicity finished for her, and Sylvia smiled.

Susan handed her the chocolate, for which Sylvia was extremely grateful, then the three girls chatted. For once, Sylvia was quiet, letting the other two do most of the talking, as she had been ordered by Matron not to strain her throat.

Susan began to tell the girl about a trick that June was planning to play on Mam'zelle Dupont the following week, but she realised that Sylvia's polite smile was becoming rather strained, and said, 'Of course, I forgot! You don't like jokes and tricks, do you, Sylvia?'

'I know it makes me seem frightfully dull and

boring, but no, I don't,' Sylvia admitted.

'It seems very odd to me,' said Felicity. 'I don't think I've ever met anyone who doesn't like jokes and tricks before.'

'Well, it's because of something that happened when I was younger,' said Sylvia.

'Did someone play a trick on you that went wrong, or hurt you?' asked Susan curiously.

'No, it was *I* who played a trick on someone else,' was Sylvia's surprising answer. 'And it went terribly wrong.'

'What happened?' asked Felicity.

'Well, I played a trick on my aunt,' said Sylvia. 'My father's younger sister. You see, we live in a big, old house, and my aunt always used to complain that it gave her the creeps. Though it never stopped her coming to stay with us! I love the house, and I became fed up of hearing her criticise it, so one night I decided that I would *really* give Aunt Aggie the creeps!'

'Whatever did you do?' asked Susan, quite unable to imagine Sylvia playing a trick.

'I dressed up as a ghost one night, and ran around in the garden under her window,' said Sylvia, looking rather ashamed now.

Felicity and Susan, with June's trick on Miss Tallant in mind, laughed, and Felicity said, 'Well, that doesn't seem so very bad.'

'Oh, but it was,' said Sylvia gravely. 'You see, Aunt Aggie was so terrified that she fainted, and banged her head as she fell. She was quite ill for a while, and had to stay with us for simply ages!'

'Heavens!' cried Felicity. 'What bad luck. But it wasn't your fault, Sylvia. I mean to say, you didn't harm your aunt on purpose.'

'No, but it quite put me off playing any tricks,' said the girl miserably.

'Yes, I can see that it would,' said Susan. 'Did you own up?'

Sylvia shook her head unhappily. 'I was too afraid,' she said guiltily. 'My aunt has quite a temper, you know, and would have been terribly angry with me. Awfully cowardly of me, I know.'

'Well, you were younger then,' said Susan, attempting to give the girl's thoughts a happier direction. 'And I'm sure that we have all done foolish things that we are not proud of at some time or other.'

Sylvia cheered up at this, and the rest of the visit passed pleasantly, until Matron came in to throw them out.

'Sylvia must rest for a little now,' she said. 'But she may have more visitors later, if some of the others would like to come.'

It was as the two girls were making their way to the common-room that Felicity suddenly stopped dead in her tracks.

'Oh, my gosh!' she cried.

'What's up?' asked Susan, looking at her in surprise.

'I've just remembered something,' said Felicity. 'Bonnie told us that Miss Tallant is afraid of ghosts because she saw one when she was younger.'

'Yes?' said Susan, a puzzled look on her face.

'And Sylvia dressed up as a ghost to frighten her aunt!' exclaimed Felicity. 'Her *aunt*, Susan! Don't you see?'

Light dawned on Susan, and she gasped. 'Olive is innocent, after all. *Sylvia* is Miss Tallant's niece.'

'Which means that Sylvia is also the sneak,' said Felicity grimly. 'Susan, we must tell the others at once.'

But while Felicity and Susan had been visiting Sylvia, a quite dreadful row had broken out in the common-room.

It started over a very little thing indeed, as big rows often do. Nora, not realising that Olive was standing behind her, had stepped back and accidentally stood on the girl's toe.

'Gosh, I'm awfully sorry, Olive!' Nora had said at once. 'I do hope that I didn't hurt you.'

'Well, you did,' snapped Olive, who seemed to be in a blacker mood than usual since she had been to see Miss Tallant. 'Why on earth can't you look where you are going?'

Nora tried to apologise again, but Olive cut her short, an unpleasant sneer on her face, as she said spitefully, 'For someone who thinks that she is *so* graceful, and *such* a marvellous dancer, you're terribly clumsy, Nora. I don't know what Susan and the others were thinking of, to let you play the fairy, for you simply aren't up to it, in my opinion.'

'Well, who cares tuppence for your opinion?' said Pam, roused to a rare show of temper by this. 'Keep it to yourself, Olive, for no one else wants to hear what you have to say.'

There were murmurs of agreement from some of the listening girls, and Olive flushed angrily. But she turned away and said no more. Things might have calmed down, if June and Freddie had not walked in at that precise moment. Sensing an atmosphere, June asked at once, 'What's the matter?'

'It's nothing,' said Nora quickly, for she had no wish to prolong the argument and just wanted to forget all about it. But Amy, who disliked Olive intensely, had other ideas, and said in her haughty way, 'Just our dear Olive causing trouble again – as usual.'

Olive turned on Amy at once, crying, 'How dare you accuse *me* of causing trouble, you horrid little snob! Nora was the one at fault, for she stood on my foot – and I wouldn't be the least bit surprised if it was deliberate!'

'Don't be ridiculous!' said Bonnie, entering the fray. 'I saw the whole thing, and it was quite obvious that it was an accident.'

'Well, you would stick up for Nora, wouldn't you?' scoffed Olive, towering over little Bonnie. 'For you are both exactly alike! Spoilt, silly, pretty little dolls!'

Then Olive folded her arms and stood with a smirk on her face, waiting for the foolish little Bonnie to burst into tears.

But she was disappointed, for Bonnie, very angry indeed, stood up to Olive, saying, 'Well, I would rather be a spoilt, silly little doll than a plain, jealous sneak! For that is what you are, Olive. And I know why you are so jealous of Nora and me, for I spoke to Annabel at half-term.'

The colour drained from Olive's face, and she hissed, 'You had no right to speak to her! No right at all!'

'I have the right to speak to anyone I please,' retorted Bonnie defiantly. 'I understand why you dislike your stepsister, Olive, I really do. I understand why you needed to cut her out of your family photograph, as though she didn't exist. But please don't take your loathing of her out on Nora and me, for it is nothing to do with us, we don't deserve it, and we don't appreciate it!'

'One up to Bonnie!' murmured June, who had been watching the scene with enjoyment. So had the others, and how they relished seeing Olive look so taken aback. There was a great deal more to Bonnie than met the eye, and Olive had found out the hard way!

Now June decided to take a hand, and she stepped forward, saying smoothly, 'Do you have any other relatives that you don't want us to know about, Olive? An aunt, for instance?'

Olive looked extremely puzzled, and said, 'I don't know what you mean.'

'Oh, I think you do,' said June. 'You see, we know all about you and Miss Tallant. We know that you have been sneaking to her, and letting her in on our secrets. What do you have to say about that, Olive?'

Olive had nothing at all to say, for she was completely speechless. But guilt was written all over her face, and she was quite unable to look any of the others in the eye. At last she opened her mouth to speak, but the only sound that came out was a little sob, and the girl ran from the room.

Olive almost knocked over Felicity and Susan, who were outside, and when Susan called out, 'Hi, Olive! Whatever is the matter?' she didn't even look round, but ran up the stairs to the dormitory.

'Well!' said Susan to Felicity, in astonishment. 'What do you suppose that was about?'

Felicity, who had glanced through the open door of the common-room and seen the grim faces of the fourth formers, thought, with a sinking heart, that she knew. She turned to Susan, and said gravely, 'I have a horrible feeling that we are too late.'

Susan gave a groan and went into the common-room, Felicity behind her.

At once June, aided by Bonnie, Nora, Pam and Amy, launched into an account of what had happened.

When they had finished, Susan groaned again, and said, 'June, I do wish that you had waited!'

'Why?' asked June, surprised and none too pleased. 'Olive was never going to own up, and as a row had already started I thought that this was the best time to tackle her.'

'But it wasn't, June,' said Felicity, looking very troubled. 'Because, you see, we have discovered that Olive is *not* Miss Tallant's niece. Sylvia is!'

There was a shocked silence, then everyone began to speak at once.

'Surely not!'

'That's impossible! I can't see Sylvia as a sneak.'

'Olive looked so guilty – it simply *must* be her.'

'And she didn't make any attempt to defend herself.'

'Well, perhaps she felt too shocked and upset to retaliate,' said Susan. 'But there is no doubt at all that Sylvia is the culprit.'

And, quickly, she told the fourth formers what she and Felicity had learned.

'I suppose it *must* be Sylvia, then,' said Pam. 'Though I'm very surprised, I must say.'

'Blow Sylvia!' said June, angrily. She felt very guilty indeed for having accused Olive unjustly, and was wishing that she had held her tongue. 'If only you had come back a few minutes earlier and told us this, Susan and Felicity, everything would have been all right.'

'Well, you can hardly blame us!' said Susan crossly, for she felt very angry with June herself. 'The fact is, that you had no right to say anything at all to Olive. As head of the form it was my duty, but, as usual, you had to take the lead, and go in all guns blazing, without thinking things through.'

June flushed angrily. She felt annoyed with herself, and annoyed with Susan. And the reason she was annoyed with Susan was because everything she said was perfectly true.

June was honest enough to admit that to herself. She *did* always have to take the lead in things. And this wasn't the first time she had caused an awkward situation by accusing someone unjustly.

Nora spoke up for her, though, saying, 'To be fair, Susan, all of us thought the same as June. We were all absolutely convinced that she was the mysterious niece, and had been sneaking to Miss Tallant. And the chances are, if June hadn't accused her to her face, one of us others would have.'

'That's very true,' said Bonnie, nodding solemnly.

'Yes, we were all feeling sore with Olive, because of the row she had started,' said Julie.

'So really we are all to blame.'

'No,' said June suddenly. 'I am to blame. Susan is quite right. I shouldn't have tackled Olive as I did. Speaking out of turn seems to be one of my biggest faults! Each time it happens I tell myself that I will think twice before doing it again, and then I go and jump in with both feet!'

'Well, at least you have the courage to own up to it,' said Felicity, admiring June for being honest enough to admit to a fault.

'Yes, but owning up to it isn't enough,' said June, ruefully. 'I need to do something to make amends. I shall go and apologise to Olive, and I will tell her that we know now that she isn't the sneak.'

Susan was a little doubtful about this, for, while she appreciated June's efforts to make it up to Olive, she wasn't sure whether the girl would accept the apology. And if Olive gave June the cold shoulder, June might flare up again, and then another quarrel would break out!

Felicity, seeing the doubt in Susan's face, said, 'I know! Why don't we all go and speak to Olive? Although she isn't the sneak, she hasn't done very much to make us think well of her, so really it's no wonder that we suspected her. But we can go to her now and tell her that we want to wipe the slate clean and give her a chance to become one of us.'

'Jolly good idea, Felicity!' cried Pam. 'Come along, everyone, let's go up to Olive now.'

So the fourth formers trooped upstairs and into the dormitory, all of them feeling rather virtuous about their decision to try and befriend Olive.

Alas for such good intentions! When Susan opened the door and the fourth formers filed in, Olive was nowhere to be seen.

'Oh!' said Susan, rather disappointed. 'She's not here. She must have come downstairs while we were talking in the common-room.'

'Perhaps she has gone for a walk in the grounds, to clear her head,' suggested Lucy.

'Yes, that's probably it,' said Julie. 'Oh well, we shall just have to wait until later to make amends to Olive.'

'There's something else,' said Freddie, looking rather serious. 'We shall have to tackle Sylvia about her behaviour.'

'Yes, I had already thought of that,' said Susan, looking rather gloomy. Bother, now there would be yet another row, and another girl sent to Coventry. She had just been getting to like Sylvia, too.

'Well, Matron said that she will probably be back in class tomorrow, so we will deal with her then. And June . . .'

June held her hands up, and said at once, 'I know, Susan! I shall leave it all to you.'

Where is Olive?

Olive did not turn up for rehearsal that afternoon, and the girls didn't see hide nor hair of her. When she failed to turn up for tea, Susan grew rather alarmed.

'I say!' she said to Felicity. 'You don't think that Olive's done anything silly, do you?'

'Whatever do you mean?' asked Felicity, startled.

'Well, it just occurred to me that she might have run away or something,' said Susan.

'Surely she wouldn't do such a thing?' said Felicity, shocked. 'Besides, where would she go? We know that she is not happy at home, so it's very unlikely that she would have gone there.'

'That makes it all the more worrying,' said Susan, with a frown. 'If she had gone home, at least we would know that she is safe.'

Pam, who had overheard this, said, 'Steady on, Susan! We don't *know* that Olive has run away. Why, for all we know she may have come back and be up in the dormitory now.'

So, after tea, Felicity and Susan, along with Pam and Nora, went up to the dormitory once more. But there was no sign of Olive.

Looking very worried indeed, Susan marched across to Olive's locker and pulled it open.

Some of her personal belongings were gone, and when Felicity took a look inside the girl's wardrobe she could see that some of her clothes were missing too.

'Oh, my word!' gasped Nora. 'It didn't seriously enter my head that she really *had* gone. Now what do we do?'

'We must report it to Miss Williams,' said Susan gravely. 'At once, for there is no time to lose!'

But Miss Williams was out, so the girls went to find Miss Potts, the head of North Tower.

She listened to their story with a very serious expression indeed, then said, 'I must inform Miss Grayling immediately. You girls had better come too, in case she needs to question you.'

So, all feeling rather nervous, the four girls followed Miss Potts to Miss Grayling's study.

The Head called to them to come in, in answer to the mistress's sharp knock, and saw at once that something was wrong.

Quickly, Miss Potts told Miss Grayling what had happened and the Head listened, her expression grave. Then she said, 'Do you girls have any idea at all where Olive may have gone?'

'None at all, Miss Grayling,' answered Susan. 'I only wish that we did.'

'Then do you know of any reason why she might have run away?' asked Miss Grayling.

The four girls looked at one another, and Miss Grayling

said, 'If you know something, it is important that you tell me, for it might help us in finding Olive.'

So Susan told the story of how the fourth formers had discovered that Miss Tallant had a niece at Malory Towers, and of how she had been sneaking to her aunt.

'We all thought it was Olive,' said Susan, rather miserably. 'And one of the girls accused her to her face. But now we know that we were wrong, and that Sylvia is Miss Tallant's niece.'

'Yes, she is,' said the Head. 'I was aware of it from the first, but at the request of both Sylvia and Miss Tallant, I kept it to myself. Both of them felt that they would be able to settle in better if no one was aware of their relationship. But we shall come back to that in a minute, for I must telephone the police at once, so that they can search for Olive.'

Miss Grayling dialled the police station and held a hurried conversation with the person at the other end of the telephone, before replacing the receiver and turning back to Miss Potts.

'Could you organise a search party of any available staff to search the grounds, please, Miss Potts?' she asked. 'The police will be here shortly, but I really don't feel that we should waste any time.'

Miss Potts nodded and left the Head's study, and Miss Grayling looked at the girls in front of her.

'Now that I know the search for Olive is in hand, let us go back to the question of Miss Tallant,' she said. 'Am I to understand that Miss Tallant has been using her position of authority to find out what you fourth formers have been up to?'

The girls looked at one another a little uncomfortably. For some of the things they had been up to were things that they did not want Miss Grayling to know about. The midnight feast, for example, and some of the tricks that June had played.

Miss Grayling saw the doubt in their faces, and smiled to herself, for she had been Head mistress at Malory Towers for many years, and guessed a little of what was going through their minds.

'I am not asking you to reveal any of your secrets to me,' she said. 'I merely want to know how Miss Tallant has been conducting herself, so that I can deal with her accordingly.'

Felicity spoke up, saying, 'Miss Grayling, it is true that Miss Tallant has found out things about the fourth form that she could not possibly have known unless she had someone spying on us. And some of us have been punished because of the things that she has found out.'

'I see,' said the Head, her face very serious. 'And yet, I find it very hard to believe that Sylvia is a sneak, for she has always struck me as a rather honest, forthright girl.'

'Yes, that is what we thought, too,' said Susan. 'We were most awfully disappointed in her when we discovered the truth.'

'But can you be sure that you know the whole story?' asked Miss Grayling. 'Just because Sylvia is Miss Tallant's niece, it does not necessarily follow that she is the one who has been giving away your secrets. In fact, the impression I received was that Sylvia and her aunt were not close at all.'

The girls looked at one another in surprise. They had been so certain that Miss Tallant's niece and the sneak were one and the same!

'Miss Grayling,' said Pam. 'Do you think it is possible that Olive *could* have been the sneak, after all? She looked awfully guilty when she was tackled, and didn't attempt to deny it.'

'It is possible,' said the Head. 'But I think the first thing to do is speak to Sylvia, so that you can be certain it is not her.'

'Will you go to her now, Miss Grayling?' asked Susan.

'Certainly not,' replied the Head. 'The police will be here at any minute, and my immediate concern is to find Olive. I am going to leave it to you, Susan, as head of the fourth form to speak to Sylvia. And I trust that you will use all the tact and wisdom that I know you possess.'

'Of course, Miss Grayling,' said Susan, feeling awfully proud that the Head thought she was tactful and wise.

Suddenly Nora, who had remained silent up until now, said, 'Miss Grayling, I think that there is something else you should know. Bonnie spoke to Olive's step-sister at half-term, and it turns out that the two of them dislike one another awfully, and there have been dreadful problems between them. I don't suppose that that has anything to do with Olive running away, but I thought I would mention it.'

'Thank you, Nora,' said Miss Grayling. 'That could prove very useful.'

Just then there came a tap at the door, and a maid announced that the police had arrived, so the fourth formers left the Head's study and went to join the others in the common-room.

There was great consternation when Susan announced that Olive had run away.

'How dreadful! I wonder where she has gone?'

'It's an awfully cold night! I do hope that she will be all right.'

'The police will find her and bring her back.'

'Well, let's hope so.'

The only person who remained silent was June. How terribly, terribly guilty she felt! If only she had held her tongue, Olive might be here now, safe and warm. Instead, she was out goodness knows where, alone in the dark and the bitter cold. If only, she, June, could make amends somehow! But perhaps she could! The others were all pre-occupied discussing Olive's disappearance and, unseen by them, June slipped from the room.

'I wonder if Matron would let me speak to Sylvia tonight?' said Susan. 'It is quite early, and I bet she is still awake.'

'Why don't you ask her?' suggested Felicity. 'I'll come with you if you like.'

So the two girls went along to the San, where Matron greeted them by saying, 'You two here again? I had no idea that you were such close friends with Sylvia.'

'Matron, we need to speak to her quite urgently,' said Felicity. 'It really is terribly important.'

Matron looked at the watch that was pinned to her crisp, white apron, and said, 'Very well. You may have twenty minutes, no more.'

Sylvia looked surprised, but very pleased, to receive a second visit from Felicity and Susan, saying, 'Hallo, there! This is a pleasant surprise.'

'Well, I hope you will think so when you hear what we have come to say, Sylvia,' said Susan. 'You see, we know that you are Miss Tallant's niece.'

'Oh,' said Sylvia, turning red. 'Well, I suppose I should have known that it would be impossible to keep it secret forever. Perhaps I should have told you all myself, at the start, but I didn't want anyone to know that I was related to her.'

Felicity and Susan noticed the distaste in Sylvia's tone, and Felicity said, 'Don't you like her, then?'

'Of course not!' said Sylvia, in surprise. 'Do you?'

'No, but she's not my aunt,' said Felicity.

'Just because you are related to someone doesn't mean that you have to like them, you know,' retorted Sylvia. 'Aunt Aggie has always been spiteful and vindictive. Even my father dislikes her, and he is her brother! They haven't spoken to one another for years. I half-expected him to take me away when I wrote and told him that Aunt Aggie was a mistress here, but he knew how much I liked it at Malory Towers, so he said that I could stay. My aunt and I bumped into each other on our first day, and – as she dislikes me every bit as much as I like her – we agreed that we would both keep quiet about being related. I told Miss Grayling, of course, for it didn't seem quite right to keep it from her.'

Felicity and Susan exchanged glances. Sylvia was being so frank and open about things, that it was harder than ever to believe that she was the sneak. Susan cleared her throat, and said, 'Sylvia, there is something I must ask you, and I do hope that you won't take offence.'

'Heavens, whatever can it be?' asked Sylvia, looking rather alarmed.

'You see, we found out some time ago that Miss Tallant had a niece in the fourth form,' explained Susan. 'And we knew that it had to be either you or Olive. And then we realised that Miss Tallant had someone in the form spying on us and reporting back to her. So we put two and two together . . .'

'And decided that the niece was also the spy,' said Sylvia, looking rather hurt. 'Well, Susan, I can assure you that I am no sneak! And even if I was, Aunt Aggie is the last person I should tell tales to!'

There was such conviction in Sylvia's voice that both girls believed her at once.

'Well,' said Felicity heavily. 'It looks as if Olive must be the culprit after all, and that is why she has run away.'

'Olive has run away!' cried Sylvia. 'My goodness, do tell me what happened.'

While Felicity and Susan were talking to Sylvia, June had slipped out into the grounds to look for Olive. She couldn't join the official search party, for Miss Potts would certainly send her back indoors, so she avoided them and hunted for Olive alone. Where *could* she be? June went to the stables, the gardener's shed, and even the changing cubicles by the swimming-pool, but there was no sign of Olive. June shivered. It really was a bitterly cold night and, in her haste to find Olive, June had not stopped to put her coat on.

Perhaps she should try searching *inside* the school, in the store-rooms or attics perhaps. It would certainly be a great deal warmer!

She heard voices – the search party approaching – and hid behind the trunk of a large tree.

'It looks as though Olive has ventured outside the school grounds,' she heard Miss Potts say heavily. 'I'm afraid we shall have to leave it to the police to search for her now. I must go and tell Miss Grayling, so that she can telephone Olive's father.'

The search party went towards the school, but June remained where she was for a moment, thinking hard. Her instincts told her that Olive was still here, at Malory Towers somewhere. And if she could be the one to find her, it would go a long way towards assuaging her feelings of guilt. Suddenly June remembered the old boat-house, down the cliff-path. It was the one place she hadn't looked, and she would be willing to bet that the search party hadn't thought of it either.

Swiftly, the girl ran across the lawn, past the swimming pool, and down the path that led to the beach. And there was the boat-house, unused now and looking very dilapidated.

June knocked on the door and called, 'Olive! Olive, are you there?'

There was no answer, and, after a moment, a dejected June was about to walk away. But then her sharp ears caught a sound – a muffled sob!

Cautiously she pushed open the door of the boat-house. A heap of old sacks lay on the floor, and there, on top of them, sat Olive, crying as if her heart would break.

June was not the most sympathetic or compassionate of girls, but she felt a pang of sorrow for poor Olive, who was obviously in great distress. Now was the time, she realised, to let her sympathy and compassion shine through, to offer help and comfort to this poor, wretched girl. So June walked forward and said, in a gentle tone, 'Come on, Olive, old girl. You really can't stay here, you know. Why don't you tell me what's up, then I'll take you back up to the school.'

'You!' cried Olive, sitting bolt upright, an expression of horror on her face. 'Go away, June! You don't care what happens to me, you just want to be the one to take me back to school to face Miss Grayling, so that all the others will say what a heroine you are!'

June felt her temper rising, but she conquered it and, flopping down on to the sacks beside Olive, said, 'You're quite wrong, you know. If you must know, I feel simply terrible about accusing you of sneaking to Miss Tallant earlier, without any real proof. I'm sorry.'

Olive stared at June, a strange expression on her face.

Then she laughed, rather wildly, and said, 'There's no need for you to apologise. You were quite right. I was sneaking to Miss Tallant.'

June stared at the girl in astonishment. 'But it is Sylvia who's the sneak! We know that now. You see, it turns out that she is Miss Tallant's niece. Are you trying to cover up for her, Olive? And, if so, why? It's not even as if the two of you are friends.'

'I'm not covering up for anyone,' said Olive, dabbing at her eyes with a crumpled handkerchief. 'I don't know anything about Sylvia being Miss Tallant's niece, but I *do* know that she wasn't the one who was sneaking to her. I was. So now you can go away and tell all the others that you were right, and that I am every bit as bad as you said I was.'

'I'm not going anywhere until I get to the bottom of this,' said June firmly. 'Olive, *why* did you spy on us for Miss Tallant? Was it just because you dislike us so?'

Olive said nothing, but merely shrugged, refusing to look June in the eye, and June felt her temper rising again. Olive really was one of the most infuriating girls she had ever met, June thought, with her odd tempers and mean, spiteful nature. Perhaps the best thing that June could do was to haul the girl back up to the school and let Miss Grayling deal with her. She looked at Olive in distaste. And, as she did so, June saw something else. She saw the misery and loneliness behind the girl's facade and, hard-hearted as she sometimes was, felt moved by it. June thought about her own behaviour during her years at

Malory Towers, and did not feel proud of some of the things she had done. Yet she had been given chance after chance to change her ways. Perhaps Olive, too, should be given a chance.

Olive, lost in her own unhappy thoughts, was most astonished when she felt an arm come round her shoulders, and heard June say rather gruffly, 'You're awfully sad, aren't you, Olive? I would like to help you, if I can. Won't you tell me what is bothering you?'

This sudden, unexpected kindness was too much for Olive, who burst into tears again, and said between sobs, 'I can't. I'm so terribly ashamed.'

'Well, we have all done things that we are ashamed of, at times,' said June, patting the girl's shoulder. 'I certainly have anyway! But the thing I have always found is that if I've done something bad, it seems to become more serious, and weigh more heavily on me, if I keep it to myself. A trouble shared is a trouble halved, and all that.'

Olive's sobs quietened a little, as she thought over what June had said. Then, at last, she turned towards the girl and said, 'Very well, I will tell you. I don't suppose it matters much if you hate me afterwards, for nobody likes me anyway!'

June said nothing to this and, after a short silence, Olive began, 'It all started with my step-sister, Annabel. From the moment that she and my step-mother moved in with Father and me, she has done nothing but cause trouble. But because she is so pretty and behaves so sweetly in front of the grown-ups, everyone believes her when she says that I am to blame. I suppose I don't help myself by flying into a rage every time I am accused of something, but I simply can't tell you how horrid and hurtful it is to be blamed for things that aren't your fault all the time.'

'I should jolly well think it would be!' exclaimed June. 'Go on, Olive.'

'Well, at first Annabel and I went to the same day school together, though she was in a different form from me, of course,' said Olive. 'And soon she started making trouble for me there too. Taking people's things and hiding them in my desk so that it looked as if I had taken them, and playing petty, mean tricks and blaming them on me.'

'What a nasty little beast she sounds,' said June. 'I'll bet that you flew into some fine rages with her!'

'I did, of course,' said Olive. 'But that only made matters worse, for everyone would leap to the defence of dear, sweet little Annabel and became more convinced than ever that I was the one in the wrong. Eventually, Father decided that I was too troublesome to stay at home, and he sent me to boarding school.'

June's heart went out to Olive as she listened. No wonder that the girl felt bitter.

'Of course, I felt terribly unhappy and terribly angry,' said Olive. 'I hated being away from home, and thinking of Annabel in my place, being spoilt by her mother and my father, and getting all of their love and attention, while I had none. That made me feel mean and spiteful, and I decided that if I was going to be sent away from home for doing horrid things, then I really *would* do them.'

'So you turned into the person that everyone had accused you of being,' said June. 'Poor old Olive!'

'Yes, but it gets much worse,' said Olive, her voice trembling a little. 'Everyone disliked me so much at that school, mistresses and girls alike. And, when I look back at my behaviour, I really can't blame them. Things came to a head when I accidentally knocked another girl, who couldn't swim, into the pool. It really *was* an accident, June, but because I had behaved so badly all year, no one believed me and I was expelled.'

June gave a gasp and Olive said, 'You're shocked. I knew that you would be.'

'I'm shocked that one spoilt, silly little girl could cause so much trouble for you,' said June in her forthright way. 'And she will go on doing so, if we don't think of a way to stop her, Olive.'

Olive felt warmed by the way June had said 'we', and suddenly she felt a little less helpless and more hopeful for the future. With someone as strong and determined as June on her side, perhaps she would find a way to outwit the sly Annabel.

'But you still haven't told me how you came to spy on us for Miss Tallant,' June said now. 'I'm very curious about that.'

'Well, I was just coming to that,' said Olive. 'You see, Miss Tallant used to teach at my old boarding school, so she knows all about the trouble I got into there, and about me being expelled. Miss Grayling knows too, but she must have seen some good in me, for she agreed to let me have a fresh start here at Malory Towers and promised to keep my secret.'

'Well!' said June, looking quite astonished. 'That explains why Miss Tallant seemed so friendly with your people at half-term. That was one of the things that made us suspect that you were her niece. Now I see that we were quite wrong, and she had already met your people at your old school.' June paused, her expression becoming hard, then went on, 'And I suppose she threatened to give your secret away unless you reported to her on all the fourth form's secrets and wrongdoing.'

Olive nodded miserably, and June's eyes flashed angrily as she said, 'Well, Miss Grayling will be very interested to hear that, and I shall take great pleasure in telling her! Olive, you really are silly! If only you had told us this from the very beginning, Miss Tallant's hold over you would have been broken.'

Olive hung her head, and said in a small voice, 'I couldn't. I felt so ashamed of myself, and I simply couldn't bear to see the scorn on everyone's faces. Oh, June, I started this term with such high hopes! I had made up my mind that I was going to settle down, and make friends, and Father would realise that I wasn't so bad after all, and would let me come home. Then the first person I met on the train was Nora, and she reminded me so much of Annabel that I simply couldn't help being rude to her. And then I found out that Miss Tallant was teaching here, and I realised that there was no point in trying to change.'

'Oh, Olive!' sighed June. 'I daresay one or two of the girls might have been a little shocked when they heard that you had been expelled, but once you had explained everything, they would have understood. And as for Miss Tallant, I feel quite certain that the Head will dismiss her immediately once she finds out what she has been up to.'

'Do you really think so?' said Olive, brightening.

'I do,' said June, getting to her feet. 'And now we had better get you back to the school, for the police are out looking for you, and I expect that Miss Grayling has telephoned your father by now.'

Olive turned pale at this, and gave a groan. 'And he will think that I have caused yet more trouble.'

'Yes, but no doubt he will be so glad that you have been found that you might not get into a row,' said June. 'In fact, I rather think that the only person who is going to get into a row is our dear Miss Tallant.'

Bonnie puts things right

Miss Grayling was most astonished, a few minutes later, when someone knocked on the door of her study, and June entered, followed by a very scared-looking Olive.

After the Head had telephoned the police to tell them that the missing girl had been found, she turned to Olive and said, 'My dear, what on earth made you run away like that? The school has been in an uproar, and your father is dreadfully worried. He is on his way here this very minute.'

'Olive, you must tell Miss Grayling everything, at once,' urged June.

So, haltingly at first, and with much prompting from June, Olive poured out the whole sorry tale.

Miss Grayling listened intently, her brow furrowing as the girl told of the spiteful way her step-sister had behaved. And when Olive spoke of the part Miss Tallant had played in her unhappiness, June noticed with satisfaction that the Head's serene blue eyes grew cold and steely.

'Well, this is a most extraordinary tale!' said Miss Grayling at last. 'Olive, you really should have come to me, or one of the other mistresses, and told us about Miss Tallant's conduct.'

'I know,' said Olive. 'But I thought that you would be certain to believe Miss Tallant's word over mine. Especially as you knew that I had been expelled from my other school for making trouble.'

'Miss Grayling, what is puzzling me is *why* Miss Tallant was so intent on finding out all our secrets,' said June, who had been looking thoughtful. 'Was it just out of spite, or did she have some other motive?'

'I rather think that Miss Tallant wanted to be offered a permanent post at Malory Towers,' said the Head. 'As you know, she is only here temporarily, whilst Miss Hibbert is ill. She has lost no opportunity to point out to me, and the other mistresses, that she thinks Miss Hibbert is a poor teacher and a poor disciplinarian. It must have been a great stroke of luck for her to discover that Olive was here. She was able to use her to find out what you fourth formers were up to, punish you, and earn herself a reputation for being strict and able to keep order.'

'Well!' cried June. 'Of all the nerve! Miss Hibbert is a splendid teacher, a million times better than Miss Tallant. She is just, and fair, her lessons are always interesting, and –'

'Quite so, June,' interrupted Miss Grayling firmly, though there was the hint of a twinkle in her eyes. 'Fortunately I have known Miss Hibbert for very many years, so a few words from a new mistress was certainly not going to change my excellent opinion of her. In fact, I will be telephoning her shortly, to see if she is well enough to come back to Malory Towers before the end of term.'

June and Olive exchanged excited glances. This was good news, and could mean only one thing – the Head was going to dismiss Miss Tallant!

'Now,' said Miss Grayling. 'Your father will be here very shortly, Olive, so I suggest you go and wash your face and hands, and brush your hair before he arrives. Then we need to talk to him about your step-sister's behaviour towards you.'

Olive's shoulders slumped, and she said glumly, 'He won't believe me. Annabel has been very convincing, you see, Miss Grayling.'

'Yes, he will!' cried June suddenly. 'I have an idea! Miss Grayling, may I be excused, please?'

'Of course,' said the Head, looking rather startled. 'Olive, you go as well, and tidy yourself up, then come straight back here.'

Both girls left the Head's study, Olive to go to the nearest bathroom, and June to go to the common-room, where the others were sitting around looking rather gloomy, as they discussed Olive's disappearance.

June burst in and Freddie cried, 'Where on earth have you been, June? We were beginning to think that you had run away too!'

'I went to look for Olive,' said June a little breathlessly, for she had run all the way to the common-room. 'And I found her. She is with the Head now.'

At once the fourth formers besieged June with questions and, as quickly as possible, she told them what had happened. The girls listened in open-mouthed silence, but they had plenty to say when June told them about Miss Tallant.

'Well, I always knew she was a horrid woman, but I had no idea she was that beastly! If only we had known, we might have been able to help poor Olive.'

'And she was scheming to take Miss Hibbert's job from her too! Lucky that the Head is so shrewd, and saw through her.'

'Thank goodness that Miss Grayling is going to dismiss her. Good riddance, I say!'

'Listen, everyone!' broke in June. 'There is another way that we can help Olive. Bonnie, you spoke to Annabel at half-term, didn't you?'

'Yes, you know that I did, for I told you so,' said Bonnie.

'And she told you, quite plainly, that she had deliberately set out to get Olive into trouble, didn't she?' said June.

'That's right,' said Bonnie, nodding.

'Good,' said June. 'Now, Bonnie, I want you to come to Miss Grayling's study with me, and tell Olive's father that. You see, Olive is afraid that he won't believe her, but you are a stranger, and what's more, you don't even *like* Olive, so you have no possible reason to lie!'

Bonnie, looking rather bewildered at the speed with which June rattled all this off, blinked and said, 'Yes, of course I shall. It's very true, I didn't like Olive at all, but as soon as I saw that Annabel was to blame for everything I began to realise that she might not be so bad underneath it all. I shall enjoy telling Olive's father what a mean little beast his step-daughter is.'

And with that, June and Bonnie left the room together. As the door closed behind them, Nora said, 'My goodness, *how* I wish that I could be a fly on the wall in Miss Grayling's study when Bonnie tells Olive's father about Annabel.'

'I'd like to be there when the Head gives Miss Tallant her marching orders,' said Felicity.

'How nice it will be to have good old Miss Hibbert back!'

Miss Grayling was seated behind her desk when June and Bonnie returned to her study, a grim-faced Mr Witherspoon and a tearful Olive sitting opposite her. The interview had not gone well, and Olive's father had brushed aside her explanation that Annabel had been to blame for everything that had gone wrong. Miss Grayling had spoken up for Olive too, but Mr Witherspoon had said gruffly, 'I accept that this Miss Tallant of yours is badly at fault, and I leave you to deal with her as I see fit. But little Annabel is a good girl, and she would never do the things that Olive is accusing her of.'

June and Bonnie arrived outside Miss Grayling's door in time to hear this, for Mr Witherspoon had a booming voice, and, as June knocked at the door, Bonnie pursed her lips.

'Come in,' called the Head, in answer to June's knock.

The two girls went in, and June said politely, 'Please, Miss Grayling, Bonnie has something that she would like to say to Mr Witherspoon.'

Mr Witherspoon looked at Bonnie and frowned. He

was a big, rather serious-looking man, and he said, 'I don't mean to be rude, young lady, but I am here on a very serious matter and I am in no mood for pleasantries.'

Bonnie smiled sweetly at him, and said in her soft voice, 'That's quite all right, Mr Witherspoon. I didn't come here to be pleasant.'

The two grown-ups and Olive looked so taken aback that it was all June could do not to burst out laughing. Mr Witherspoon opened his mouth to retort, but Bonnie spoke first, saying, 'I don't know why you should believe Annabel over your own daughter, but I am here to tell you that Olive is speaking the truth. You see, I spoke to your step-daughter Annabel at half-term, and she boasted to me that she has been doing mean tricks to get Olive into trouble.'

There was a note of doubt in Mr Witherspoon's voice now, as he said, 'Are you sure that you're not saying this to get your friend out of trouble?'

'Olive isn't my friend,' said Bonnie. 'She has been mean and horrible to me since the day we met, because I remind her of Annabel. But I'm not like Annabel at all inside, for I don't lie. And, now that you can see that I have no reason at all to be nice to Olive, I hope that you will believe me.'

Mr Witherspoon looked completely dumbfounded by this, and Miss Grayling said, 'Thank you for coming and telling us this, Bonnie. The two of you may go now.'

June and Bonnie turned, but Mr Witherspoon got to his feet and said, 'Just a minute! I'd like to thank you as well, Bonnie. You're a very outspoken and courageous young lady. And my Olive may not have been very nice to you, but you have been a good friend to her today. And you jolly well put me in my place too! Now I can see that I'm going to have to make things up to Olive, otherwise I shall have you after me again!'

'Bonnie, you were simply splendid!' said June, once they were outside in the corridor. 'Olive should be very grateful to you, and if she isn't, then I, for one, will wash my hands of her!'

But Olive was grateful. Very grateful indeed! She came into the common-room an hour later, her face glowing with pleasure, looking so happy that the others could hardly believe she was the same girl.

She stood on the threshold for a moment, smiling shyly round, then, spotting Bonnie, she made straight for her, and gave the surprised girl a great big hug.

'Bonnie, I simply can't thank you enough!' she cried. 'Everything has come right, and it's all thanks to you.'

Bonnie smiled and said slyly, 'I didn't do too badly for a silly little doll, did I?'

Olive flushed and said, 'I could kick myself for calling you that. I take it back, and I apologise. Please say that you forgive me!'

'You're forgiven,' said Bonnie. 'But only if you tell us what happened with your father.'

'He was quite overcome with remorse,' said Olive. 'And simply couldn't apologise enough for doubting my word and believing Annabel all the time. He is going to talk to my step-mother when he gets home, and Annabel is in for the scolding of her life tomorrow.'

'Well, she certainly deserves it,' said Susan. 'I just hope that she learns something from it, and changes her ways.'

'She had better, for Father said that he isn't going to stand any nonsense from her,' said Olive with a grin. 'And the best of it is, that I am to go home when term ends, and go back to my old day school.'

'Well, I like that!' said Pam, in dismay. 'You've just changed for the better, and gone all friendly and jolly, and now you tell us that you're leaving!'

'I daresay you will all be glad to see the back of me,' said Olive rather gruffly. 'I can't blame you, for I've been quite unbearable.'

'Yes, you have,' said June in her usual blunt manner. 'But at least we know that there was a reason for it. And we don't want you becoming unbearable again, for this new, happy Olive is much more likeable than the old one, and she is the one we want to spend the rest of the term with.'

'Hear, hear!' cried Felicity.

'Thanks awfully,' said Olive, looking quite pretty now that she was smiling and her eyes were shining with happiness. 'I promise that I shan't go back to my old ways.'

'Well, we're jolly glad to hear it,' said Nora, who had also suffered badly from Olive's rudeness.

Olive remembered this now, and said, 'I owe you an apology too, Nora, and you, Felicity, and ... oh, it will probably take me the whole night if I apologise to everyone one by one, so I'll just say a great big SORRY to you all!'

The others laughed at this, and Olive said, 'I say, Miss Tallant was walking towards Miss Grayling's study when I left. I shouldn't be a bit surprised if she's packing her bags this very minute.'

A great cheer went up at this, and Felicity said, 'What a day it's been! But Miss Tallant leaving will just round it off perfectly.'

The Christmas concert

'Come along, everyone! Places, please!' called Susan.

It was the afternoon before the end-of-term concert, and the fourth formers were having a dress rehearsal for their play.

'Doesn't everything look splendid?' said Felicity happily.

'Yes, the scenery looks absolutely super,' said Sylvia.

'And Bonnie has done a marvellous job with the costumes,' said Susan. 'I don't see how our play can fail to be a hit.'

'It's going to be a wonderful ending to the term,' said Felicity. 'At last everything seems to be going right for us. Olive has changed her ways and become one of us now, Miss Tallant has gone, Miss Hibbert is back and everything is working out perfectly!'

Miss Tallant had left Malory Towers the morning after Olive had run away, and the fourth formers had watched her go from their common-room window.

'Good riddance!' Freddie had said with satisfaction.

'Yes, she is undoubtedly the most unpopular mistress Malory Towers has ever had,' Felicity had said. 'I, for one, won't miss her.'

Sylvia, released from the San by Matron, had added,

'Now perhaps you can understand why I didn't want to admit that she is my aunt. I feel quite ashamed to be related to her. Especially now that I know how she treated poor Olive.'

Olive had clapped Sylvia on the back and said, 'There's no need for *you* to be ashamed, Sylvia, old girl. It wasn't your fault.'

Miss Hibbert had taken a keen interest in the fourth formers' play, but unlike Miss Tallant she had not pushed herself forward or tried to take over. Instead, she had let it be known that she was willing to help if she was needed, and had remained in the background.

'Because Miss Hibbert is a jolly good teacher,' Susan had said. 'And she understands that we are going to learn far more if we do this for ourselves.'

Now the actors trooped on to the stage, and the three producers felt a thrill of pride.

There was Lucy in her teddy-bear costume and Julie, dressed as the toy soldier. Little Molly looked very sweet in her white nightdress, while Pam, wearing a grey wig and an apron, made a very convincing old lady. As for Nora, she looked very pretty indeed in her fairy costume, and Bonnie fussed round her, arranging the skirt and making sure that the wings were in position.

At last everyone was ready, and Susan called out, 'Righto, we are going to do the whole play from beginning to end, so I hope that everyone is word perfect. Olive, are you ready, just in case anyone forgets her lines?'

Olive – a cheerful, friendly Olive – had volunteered to

act as prompter, and was sitting in the wings now with her script at the ready.

'I'm here, Susan!' she called cheerily.

And the rehearsal began. It wasn't *quite* perfect, for Julie tripped over during the dance, Pam forgot one of her lines and Mary, at the piano, dropped her music on the floor and lost her place. But the most worrying thing was Molly. She knew all her lines perfectly, and didn't make any mistakes, but she had been suffering from a sore throat and her voice was little more than a croak.

'Oh dear!' said Felicity, sounding very worried. 'I wouldn't be surprised if Molly lost her voice altogether by tomorrow.'

'Don't say that!' begged Susan. 'Why, if that happens we shan't be able to perform our play, for no one could possibly learn all of Molly's lines and take her place at such short notice.'

'I'm sure that she will be perfectly fine,' said Sylvia, trying her hardest to sound optimistic. 'Why, I had a sore throat myself just recently, but after a couple of days in the San I was as right as rain.'

'But we don't have a couple of days,' said Felicity. 'Our play is tomorrow!'

But, as the day wore on, poor Molly's throat became steadily worse, until she could hardly speak at all, and after tea Miss Williams came to the common-room, with bad news.

'Girls, I'm awfully sorry, but I have just heard that Molly has been taken to the San. Miss Grayling has telephoned her parents and, as it is the last day of term tomorrow, they are coming to take her home in the morning.'

There was consternation at this, of course. Everyone felt terribly sorry for Molly, for they knew how much she had wanted her mother and father to see her perform. But they were also very concerned about their play.

'June, you must do it!' said Felicity. 'You have a better memory than anyone in the form, and if anyone can learn the lines in time you can.'

'I might have a good memory, but I couldn't possibly learn all those lines in time,' said June, quite horrified. 'What about asking Molly's friend Harriet? I know that she helped Molly to learn her lines, so she must know them very well.'

'Yes, but Harriet can't act for toffee,' said Sylvia. 'And she's far too tall to play a little girl.'

'Yes, the costume would never fit her,' said Bonnie. 'And I don't have time to make another.'

'Then what is to be done?' asked Felicity in despair. 'We have all worked so hard on this play. We simply can't abandon it now.'

'There's no question of abandoning it,' said Susan, a determined note in her voice. 'Olive, you will have to play the part of Amelia.'

'Me?' squeaked Olive. 'Oh, Susan, I couldn't possibly!'

'You must,' said Susan. 'You know the part, for you have been acting as prompter. And you're only slightly taller than Molly, so the costume should fit you.'

'But we don't even know if Olive can act,' pointed out Sylvia.

'Well, we'll soon find out,' said Susan. 'Olive, stand up and do the scene where the fairy doll comes to life, with Nora.'

Rather reluctantly, Olive got to her feet, and she and Nora acted out the scene. Olive was very hesitant at first, and her voice shook. But gradually she became more confident, and proved to the others that she wasn't a bad little actress at all.

'We're saved!' cried Felicity joyously, as the little scene came to an end and the others clapped. 'Olive, you'll be marvellous.'

'I don't know that I will,' said Olive, turning pink at the applause. 'I mean to say, it's one thing to act out a little scene in here, in front of you others, but it will be quite different standing up on stage in front of an audience full of parents and mistresses and doing a whole play.'

'The whole form will be in your debt if you do it, Olive,' said Susan.

'Yes, and think how pleased and proud your father and step-mother will be when they watch you playing one of the leading roles,' said Pam.

'And it will be one in the eye for that nasty little Annabel,' said Bonnie. 'She won't like the fact that you are the centre of attention, for once, and not her.'

Olive laughed at this, and said, 'Well, it seems as if I have three very good reasons for doing it. And, apart from my nerves, I can't think of a single reason to refuse.'

Of course, the fourth formers were thrilled to hear this, and everyone gathered round Olive, patting her on the back.

'Good show, Olive! You've really saved our bacon.'

'You'll be absolutely super, you'll see.'

'Yes, you'll bring the house down.'

'And perhaps we can fit an extra rehearsal in tomorrow morning,' said Felicity. 'Just so that you feel more confident.'

Just then the bell went for bedtime and Susan said, 'Come along, everyone. We all need to get a good night's sleep, for we have a very busy day tomorrow.'

And it certainly was a busy day! There were no proper lessons, for the three top forms were busy with preparations for the show. The lower forms felt very happy to have a free day, and spent their time peeping into the hall to watch last-minute rehearsals, and getting under everyone's feet.

'Silly kids,' said Susan rather loftily, after she had sent two giggling first formers packing for laughing at Lucy in her teddy-bear costume. 'Righto, let's try that scene once more.'

Lunch and tea that day were very makeshift affairs, for the kitchen staff were fully occupied with the sumptuous supper that they were preparing for the parents that evening.

'Bread and jam,' said Nora in disgust, at the tea-table. 'I say, Bonnie, where did you get that cake from? No one else has a piece!'

'I slipped into the kitchen and Cook gave it to me,' said Bonnie, with her angelic smile. 'I told her that I was simply *starving* and felt quite faint.'

'Trust you to get your own way, Bonnie!' said Olive. But she was laughing, and there was no bitterness in her voice, as there would have been a short while ago. Once again, the girls marvelled at how much she had changed.

'I feel quite sorry that Olive will be leaving tomorrow,' said Felicity to Susan. 'She really is a good sort now that she has settled down.'

'Yes,' said Susan. 'It seems funny now to think that none of us were keen on the two new girls when they first started. But both of them have turned out fine.'

'Yes, Sylvia even seems to have found her sense of humour now that her aunt has gone,' said Felicity. 'Do you know, she actually told me a joke yesterday!'

Susan laughed, and said, 'She'll be playing tricks on Mam'zelle Dupont before we know where we are.'

At last it was seven o'clock and time for the concert to begin. The parents had already arrived and taken their seats in the big hall, along with the mistresses and the lower school. The fourth formers sat with them for the first part of the concert, for they were on last, and they watched the sixth formers perform their Christmas readings.

'Awfully boring,' murmured Amy to Bonnie. 'I'm surprised the parents haven't fallen asleep!'

The fourth formers clapped politely as the reading drew to a close, then, as the fifth formers walked on to the stage, they slipped quietly from their seats and went backstage, to prepare for their play.

Bonnie darted about all over the place, making sure that everyone looked as perfect as possible, while Amy had graciously agreed to help with the hair and make-up. The three producers dealt ably with attacks of last-minute nerves, keeping everyone's spirits up, while the actors themselves muttered their lines under their breath, quite determined that they were not going to forget a single word.

At last the last bars of 'Silent Night' faded away, the sound of clapping could be heard, and it was time for their play to begin. The scenery was already in place, and the actors walked on to the stage.

There were gasps of delight from the first and second formers as they stared at Nora, dressed as a fairy, Lucy sitting on the floor in her teddy-bear costume, and Julie, standing to attention as the toy soldier.

Then Olive, as Amelia, appeared, looking rather shy and scared, but when she spoke the play's opening lines, her nerves seemed to disappear.

Miss Grayling, in the front row, glanced across at Mr and Mrs Witherspoon, smiling to herself when she saw the proud looks on their faces. Mr Witherspoon looked as if he was about to burst! Beside them sat a scowling Annabel, who didn't seem to be enjoying the little play at all!

But Annabel was the only one, for the rest of the audience enjoyed it enormously, and agreed among themselves that it was the best part of the concert.

'Everything is going marvellously,' said Felicity to Susan, as the two of them, with Sylvia, watched from the wings. 'Olive is giving a splendid performance.'

'I knew that she would,' said Susan happily. 'And Nora looks lovely.'

'I say, look at Mam'zelle, in the second row,' whispered Sylvia. 'She's thoroughly enjoying herself!'

Nora and Olive were acting out one of the humorous moments in the play that June and Freddie had written, and the audience were laughing very loudly. But no one laughed louder than Mam'zelle, whose cries of mirth made heads turn in her direction.

'Dear old Mam'zelle!' said Felicity fondly.

Then came the song and dance routine, which almost brought the house down, and at last the play was over. There was silence for a moment, then clapping and cheering broke out from the audience, and, thrilled, Susan said, 'They liked it! They didn't cheer like that for the fifth and sixth formers.'

'They more than liked it – they loved it!' said Felicity happily.

'Yes, I think we've done a jolly good job as producers,' said Sylvia. 'If I do –'

'IF YOU DO SAY SO YOURSELF!' chorused Felicity and Susan, then the three girls burst into laughter.

The cast took another bow, then the curtain came down and everyone ran off-stage, as the applause died away.

'We had better help them get changed, then we can go and join our people for supper,' said Susan. 'I'm jolly hungry, for lunch and tea were pretty poor.'

June and Freddie were also backstage, helping to hang up the costumes as the girls who had acted in the play got changed.

'I think that we can count that as a success,' said Freddie happily.

'Yes, and that is largely due to you and June,' said Felicity. 'The jokes that you wrote made everyone laugh.'

June seemed unusually quiet and pensive, and Susan asked, 'Anything wrong, June?'

'No, I'm just rather sorry that this term is almost at an end,' said June with a sigh. 'It hasn't all been good, but on the whole it has been fun. Next term won't be, for we shall all be studying for School Cert. And after that, we go up into the fifth. No tricks, no jokes, and no feasts then! We shall have to go all serious and dignified.'

'Well, we have a couple more terms in which to learn to be serious and dignified,' said Felicity with a laugh. 'And I daresay we shall find other ways of having fun. My sister Darrell and your cousin Alicia certainly did.'

'Yes, that's true,' said June, brightening a little. 'Alicia was as bold and bad as I am when she was younger. Yet she turned into a good, responsible top former. But she kept her sense of fun too, and that is what I want to do.'

'You will,' Felicity assured her. 'I can't imagine a serious, sober June!'

'Home for the hols tomorrow!' said Susan happily. 'What fun it will be, and the concert was a simply super way to end the term.'

'Yes,' said Felicity, with a contented sigh. 'A marvellous way to say goodbye to Malory Towers.'

And now we must say goodbye to Malory Towers too, for the moment, but we will come back when Felicity and her friends are in the fifth form.

Don't miss the next Malory Towers story ...

Enid Blyton

Malory Towers

Fun and Games

Written by Pamela Cox

There's tension in the fifth form – Millicent
keeps arranging orchestra rehearsals to clash
with June's tennis matches. But the girls
soon find there's more to worry about when
belongings start disappearing from dorms.

Don't miss the next Malory Towers story ...

Enid Blyton

Malory Towers

Secrets

Written by Pamela Cox

Malory Towers is full of secrets this term.
How did Daffy pull off her latest prank?
What did Mam'zelle find in her handbag?
And why is the girls' new form-mate
so familiar?

Look out for more classic school stories from

Enid Blyton

ST CLARE'S

Schooldays at St Clare's are never dull
for twins Pat and Isabel O'Sullivan
and their friends.

There's mischief at St Clare's!

More classic stories from the world of

Enid Blyton

The Naughtiest Girl

Elizabeth Allen is spoilt and selfish. When she's
sent away to boarding school she makes up her mind
to be the naughtiest pupil there's ever been! But
Elizabeth soon finds out that being bad isn't as
simple as it seems. Thre are ten brilliant books
about the Naughtiest Girl to enjoy.